DEATH AT COFFEE BREAK

Coffee break was going strong in the art department.

Students and staff jostled each other in the cramped space. With loud hilarity and noisy enthusiasm they gossiped and argued. Only an event of extraordinary magnitude could quell that remarkable din. . . .

Suddenly a door opened and a man staggered into the room.

"Help me!" he gasped hoarsely. "Oh, my God, I'm dying!"

Bantam Books offers the finest in classic and modern American mystery stories. Ask your bookseller for the books you have missed.

Stuart Palmer
Murder on the Blackboard
Rex Stout
Broken Vase
Death of a Dude
Death Times Three
Fer-de-Lance
The Final Deduction
Gambit
The Rubber Band
Too Many Cooks
The Black Mountain
Max Allan Collins
The Dark City
William Kienzle
The Rosary Murders
Joseph Louis
Madelaine
The Trouble with Stephanie
coming soon: Desert Heat
M.J. Adamson
Not Till a Hot January
A February Face
Remember March
April When They Woo
coming soon: May's Newfangled
Mirth
Conrad Haynes
Bishop's Gambit, Declined
Perpetual Check
Barbara Paul
First Gravedigger
But He Was Already Dead
When I Got There
P.M. Carlson
Murder Unrenovated
Rehearsal for Murder
Ross Macdonald
The Goodbye Look
Sleeping Beauty
The Name Is Archer
The Drowning Pool
The Underground Man
The Zebra-Striped Hearse
The Ivory Grin
Margaret Maron
The Right Jack
Baby Doll Games
One Coffee With

William Murray
When the Fat Man Sings
Robert Goldsborough
Murder in E Minor
Death on Deadline
The Bloodied Ivy
Sue Grafton
"A" Is for Alibi
"B" Is for Burglar
"C" Is for Corpse
"D" Is for Deadbeat
R.D. Brown
Hazzard
Villa Head
Joseph Telushkin
The Unorthodox Murder of
Rabbi Wahl
The Final Analysis of Doctor
Stark
coming soon: An Eye for an Eye
Richard Hilary
Snake in the Grasses
Pieces of Cream
Pillow of the Community
coming soon: Behind the Fact
Carolyn G. Hart
Design for Murder
Death on Demand
Something Wicked
coming soon: Honeymoon with
Murder
Lia Matera
Where Lawyers Fear to Tread
A Radical Departure
The Smart Money
coming soon: Hidden Agenda
Robert Craig
The Monkey's Raincoat
Keith Peterson
The Trapdoor
There Fell A Shadow
Jim Stinson
Double Exposure
Carolyn Wheat
Where Nobody Dies
Marilyn Wallace
Primary Target

Margaret Maron

ONE COFFEE WITH

BANTAM BOOKS
TORONTO · NEW YORK · LONDON · SYDNEY · AUCKLAND

This edition contains the complete text
of the original hardcover edition.
NOT ONE WORD HAS BEEN OMITTED.

ONE COFFEE WITH

A Bantam Book / published by arrangement with the author

PRINTING HISTORY
Raven House edition published December 1982
Bantam edition / September 1988

ISBN 0-553-27479-1

Published simultaneously in the United States and Canada

Bantam Books are published by Bantam Books, a division
of Bantam Doubleday Dell Publishing Group, Inc. Its trademark, consisting of the words "Bantam Books" and the por-
trayal of a rooster, is Registered in U.S. Patent and Trademark
Office and in other countries. Marca Registrada. Bantam
Books, 666 Fifth Avenue, New York, New York 10103.

PRINTED IN THE UNITED STATES OF AMERICA

O   0 9 8 7 6 5 4 3 2 1

For Joe

1

Few institutions of higher learning are content that their faculties do nothing but teach. In the name of "academic community," Administration arranges committees, faculty-student teas, receptions to meet the newest trustee, and interdisciplinary seminars. Departments that submit to this nonsense unquestioningly are rewarded with buildings of their own or, at the very least, whole floors of contiguous classrooms and well-furnished offices.

In every college, though, there is always one department that doesn't give a damn for academic community, that adopts a laissez-faire attitude toward Administration's extracurricular entanglements and subsequently finds itself jammed higgledy-piggledy into the college's leftover spaces.

The Art Department at Vanderlyn College was so thoroughly a case in point that when rumors of murder first spread across campus that spring morning, the other less flamboyant disciplines sat back in smug conviction that such a calamity could never happen in *their* orderly domains. Psychology alluded darkly to the dangers of indulging Freudian aggressions, Chemistry proclaimed itself appalled that lethal substances had been treated with such casual negligence, while Home Ec. polished its elegant china tea service and managed to imply that that's what came of drinking cafeteria coffee from a Styrofoam cup.

2

The day began normally enough.

Although financially besieged on all sides, New York still offered her resident, subway-riding children an education that was virtually free. Vanderlyn was one of eleven senior colleges that formed the City University of New York, and its enrollment alone was more than forty thousand, counting undergraduate, graduate and evening students.

Built in the late nineteenth century when the city still had open spaces around its edges, Vanderlyn College occupied what was now a rather expensive slice of urban real estate two blocks wide by eight blocks long. It resembled any other institution of higher learning, except that none of its stone or brick buildings was a dormitory or faculty residence. There was the obligatory grassy common crossed by patterned brick walks with a large fountain in its center; there were tall oaks and maples and a curtain of ivy to soften the north wall of the ugly old late-Victorian library; there was even a postage-stamp-sized athletic field tucked in next to the East River and a graceful trellised promenade, draped in wisteria, from which one could watch the river traffic float by while catching up on obscure battles in the Hundred Years War.

Spring sunlight fell on sleepy-eyed students straggling up from the subway's depths and through the iron gates to eight-o'clock classes, while on the third floor of Van Hoeen Hall, Assistant Professor Marvin Lowenheim (B.A., Pittsburgh; M.A., Michigan; Ph.D., Columbia) readied himself to face a cowed class of freshmen. Years of conducting English Composition 1.2 at eight o'clock in the morning had transformed a gentle Spenser scholar into a tyrannical martinet, who frowned as he distributed rigorously graded compositions.

"It seems we shall need more drill on 'Unity and Coherence in Paragraph Construction,' " he told them grimly.

Another ordinary Wednesday morning had begun.

The art department began Wednesday morning normally enough by following its own eccentric course. Just after eight o'clock a large open truck arrived at the side of Van Hoeen Hall by way of the service road that circled the campus. From the fourth-floor window above the truck, a thick steel bar extended itself hydraulically. A heavy-duty block-and-tackle apparatus was attached to its end, and as a steel cable was let down to the truck bed, a small crowd gathered to watch the fun.

The driver of the truck was a wiry young black man who wore faded slacks, a ragged sweatshirt, and expensive polarized sunglasses. He scrambled out of the cab and onto its top to direct a pickup crew composed of his two best students and several coveralled workmen from Buildings and Grounds.

"Watch it, baby!" he yelled. "The padding's slipped, and the cable's going to scar the *H*."

The girl student, redheaded, freckled and agile in beat-up sneakers and blue jeans, readjusted the padding. "You're acting like a nervous daddy in an obstetrics ward, Sam," she gibed. "Quit worrying. We haven't lost a piece of sculpture yet."

"Nor a sculptor," grinned her classmate, a tall blond youth, who stood in the open window above, awaiting his instructor's signal to haul away.

Sam Jordan (Instructor, Sculpture and Predental) was not amused. He personally checked the cable's fastening and secured the guy rope, which he tossed to one of the workmen standing on the ground. Then he climbed back up to his perch on the truck cab and anxiously surveyed the scene.

"Okay, take it up, but for crissake go easy," he commanded.

Slowly and ponderously the heavy steel object rose into the air. Sunlight glittered on its mirror-bright surfaces, then gasps followed by snickers arose from the surrounding loungers as they realized that the piece of sculpture consisted of four six-foot-tall letters welded together into a graphic expletive whose meaning was totally at variance with the sculpture's immaculate surface sheen.

"Hey, man! More tension on the guy rope!" Jordan shouted as the steel letters swung too near Van Hoeen's rough stone wall.

Up past the first floor, then past the second, floated the massive word.

"What's going on here?" suddenly demanded a querulous voice.

Sam Jordan looked down to see the deputy chairman of his department, Professor Riley Quinn, regarding the operation with distaste.

"You speaking to me?" he asked belligerently from atop the truck's cab.

"Ah, Jordan. Of course!" said Professor Quinn with acid geniality. "I should have recognized this newest addition to your oeuvre. Polished steel! Does this represent a shift away from—let's see now—I believe you called it 'the uncompromised honesty' of black iron?"

The deputy chairman was of medium height and wore a hat that shaded his eyes quite as effectively as Jordan's sunglasses. He was always exquisitely groomed and tailored and, even when physically looking up at someone, managed to give the impression of looking down his nose. He was doing it now, a sardonic smile on his lips as he said, "I thought I should make sure this was a legitimate piece being taken up to the gallery." He paused two beats. "Nevertheless, don't let me interrupt you."

Before Jordan could find a reply, Professor Quinn noticed that the workman on the guy rope had slackened his hold, and that the sculptured word hovered dangerously close to the wall.

"You there! Watch what you're doing!" he ordered sharply.

The workman turned and glared at him. "Who you think you bossing what to do?" he cried in heavily accented anger.

"Oh, God!" groaned Quinn, recognizing nemesis in brown coveralls.

"Yah! You should call on God to forgive you!" agreed the workman.

"Listen, you dumb hunky! Watch what you're doing!" cried the suddenly enraged Quinn.

"You call *me* hunky! You dare, you—you thieving *fattyú!*"

Sam Jordan was startled by the usually urbane Riley Quinn's loss of composure. This supposedly lofty academic had spoken like a common guttersnipe. But the situation was too perilous to worry about minor cracks in the deputy chairman's facade.

"What the hell's going on!" he yelled at the workman. "Will you watch what you're doing?"

He was too late.

The dot of the sculpture's lowercase *i* was a fifteen-pound hollow metal ball that hung from the left crossbar of the capital *T* by a slender three-foot chain. As the enraged workman shook his fist at Professor Quinn, the chain began to swing like a pendulum. The dot, now converted into a miniature wrecking ball, crashed through a third-floor window, putting a halt to Professor Lowenheim's remarks on unity and coherence.

"See what you make me do?" screamed the workman. "I kill you for this! I punch your nose in, you *rohadt alak!*"

A fellow worker from Buildings and Grounds blocked the workman's furious lunge toward Riley Quinn, and the red-haired girl rushed for the guy rope before the steel dot could do further damage.

"I'll have you fired!" Professor Quinn promised, al-

most purple now with answering rage. "I've endured all
the threats and insults from you that I intend to take!"

Laughter, catcalls and applause from the surrounding windows followed the deputy chairman's stormy
withdrawal from the field of battle.

Thus the arrival of the first piece of artwork for the
Art Department's spring faculty exhibition.

At that point, Wednesday morning stopped being
normal at Vanderlyn College. Especially for the Art
Department.

3

In a department rampant with egoists, eccentrics and aesthetes, the chairman's secretary, Sandy Keppler, was sensible, efficient and decorative, with long blond hair, fair skin and a smile that began in blue eyes and ended in devastating dimples. But even her considerable tact and charm were taxed by the effort of soothing Professor Quinn's ruffled feathers when he came storming into the Art Department offices on the seventh floor of Van Hoeen Hall shortly after eight-thirty.

Sandy listened to him rage and then put through his telephone call to the office of Buildings and Grounds. Before long Quinn's voice could be heard repeating stridently, "S-z-a-b-o. Szabo! Mike Szabo. The man's a lunatic! Every time I turn around, there he is, accusing me of the most incredible actions. I want him fired. Yes, I'm aware that unions—yes, I know about due process—damn it, I *do* have sufficient grounds! Haven't you been listening?"

The official in Buildings and Grounds might have been inattentive, but those members of the department who had come to work early were all ears, drifting in and out of Sandy's office on flimsy pretexts. Quinn was usually such an imperturbable bastard. A born critic and as such, little loved, he was sharp-tongued and thick-skinned; very seldom could anyone slip a needle under that armor. How a clumsy workman with broken English could make him fall apart was a question that puzzled almost everyone, especially the junior members who didn't know Mike Szabo's history.

It did not puzzle Piers Leyden, however. Not only did Leyden (Assistant Professor, Life Painting) know why

7

Quinn was irritated by the very sight of Mike Szabo, it was Leyden who had spoken to a crony over at Buildings and Grounds and caused Szabo to be hired. He had done it deliberately and with malice aforethought, and now he stood in Sandy's office enjoying the fruits of his labors.

Quinn caught sight of Leyden's grinning face through the open office door and with a visible effort drew himself together.

"An interesting phenomenon, laughter," he observed coldly. "I shall certainly have to incorporate more of it myself in my new book."

Quinn's comment was a pointed reminder of the power he, as a critic, had to make or break artistic careers.

It was Leyden's turn to glower.

Sandy managed to prevent open warfare by reminding Quinn of his nine-o'clock class, but when he popped back in at nine-fifty for the slides he needed for his ten-o'clock lecture, he was still in such waspish temper that he insulted two more of his colleagues and sent a graduate assistant home in tears.

By ten-twenty-five, though, the floor was quiet, things seemed almost normal, and Sandy felt she could safely start on her usual trip to the cafeteria for coffee. Although she was really secretary only to the chairman, Oscar Nauman, Sandy considered the whole department her responsibility. She sheltered its people from Administration's hectoring; she typed their essays for scholarly art journals and their subsequent angry rebuttals to the editors of those same journals; she listened with amusement to their jokes and with sympathy to their diatribes; and—as with her intercession between Leyden and Quinn earlier—she trod a fine impartial line between the studio artists and the art historians.

In that uneasy coexistence Sandy Keppler's artful curves were one subject both factions could usually agree on, although Piers Leyden, a neo-realist, thought she could have modeled for Fragonard, while Dumont, a baroque specialist, argued for Tiepolo. It was a spirited battle, but since Sandy's heart belonged to David Wade, one of the young untenured lecturers, discussion of her body remained purely academic.

To add to her charms, she did as favors tasks that others might have considered demeaning. She wanted a midmorning cup of coffee, and she wanted to drink it in her big, shabby office amid rowdy, disputatious staff and students, so why should she be selfish about it? As long as it was her choice and not something demanded, Sandy was quite willing to fetch refreshments for anyone else.

As she skimmed down the hall to the elevator, she was intercepted by Associate Professor Albert Simpson (Classical Art History) and Lemuel Vance (Associate Professor, Printmaking), who both fumbled in their pockets for change. Vance wanted hot chocolate.

"Tea for you, Professor?" asked Sandy.

"No, I think I'll have coffee today," said Professor Simpson. "Black with one sugar, please."

Lemuel Vance couldn't resist the gleam of Sandy's long bare legs beneath a spring green cotton skirt.

"Summer must be 'icumen in,' " he grinned. "Those are the first female legs I've seen since last fall."

Vance knew all about the practical aspects of pants —their comfort, their convenience, their warmth in cold weather—and one always ran the risk of being called a chauvinist if one expressed a simple admiration of female anatomy, but how lovely were young girls in spring dresses! The pale green and gold of her reminded him of Botticelli's Venus, and he was unwisely tempted into a classical allusion. "You look as fresh as Aphrodite when she was first fashioned from sea spray!"

Professor Simpson could never let a classical misapprehension go uncorrected. "Actually she wasn't formed from sea spray, you know," he told Vance kindly. "If you'll recall, Cronus mutilated his father, Uranus, and flung the—"

Belatedly the elderly historian remembered that

Sandy was a living, breathing girl, not a mythological abstraction. Unwilling to elaborate further on Cronus's unfilial behavior, he broke off in old-fashioned reticence.

Vance waited questioningly. "Flung what where?" he prompted.

"I'll lend you a book," Simpson said austerely and moved away.

Sandy slipped into the elevator, choking back laughter at Lemuel Vance's blank look. She knew exactly what part of Uranus's anatomy Cronus had thrown into the sea. David had explained the birth of Aphrodite very graphically once. Still, it was sweet of Professor Simpson to be too embarrassed to recount the three-thousand-year-old tale in mixed company.

On the first floor she picked up the department's morning mail, then walked downstairs to a snack bar adjoining the main cafeteria. There was the usual assortment of students: some munched corn muffins and worked crossword puzzles with buttery fingers; others sipped weak tea and idled away the time in conversation till their next classes; still another, a determinedly solitary girl, hunched over a chart of French conjugations with the desperate and fatalistic air of one who had flunked too many pop quizzes.

At the rear of the deep room three smaller tables had been pushed into a single long one, and there a number of the clerical-administrative staff sat together with their backs against the wall, openly dissecting everyone who passed. Middle-aged women all, most were plump, beringed and elaborately coiffed and made-up. They delighted in red tape, deadlines and all regulations pertaining to IBM grade cards, and their exasperated sighs when asked to perform any service out of the routine could chill newly appointed faculty members. Only half in jest they agreed that Vanderlyn would be an ideal place to work if one could dispense with the teachers and students.

Unlike them, Sandy liked most of the students and considered her own charges on Art's faculty rather fun.

Still, she was savvy enough to realize how difficult those career secretaries could make her job if they chose not to cooperate with her in interdepartmental business, so she was careful not to appear rude even when avoiding them. She waggled her fingers in friendly greeting as she passed but continued on to the service counter, aware of their neutral eyes on her progress.

The line at the counter was short; and as the five cups of hot beverages were placed on her tray, Sandy scrawled an abbreviated note of each cup's contents across its plastic snap-on lid with a felt-tipped pen: coffee with sugar—C/W/SUG; chocolate—CHOC; coffee black—BLK. Heading back toward the door, she spotted a familiar profile and detoured to the table.

"Hi, Andrea. You're in early today."

Andrea Ross (Assistant Professor, Medieval Art History) looked up from her sketchy breakfast and smiled at the girl, ruefully aware of her own passing youth. Not yet thirty, she was only now acquiring chic; never again would her thin face hold the spring-fresh appeal of Sandy's open prettiness. Still her career offered compensations. Or it had until recently, she thought with another flare of well-concealed anger.

"I've got to pull slides for my eleven o'clock, but if you want company, I'll wait," Andrea offered.

"No, I'm going back, too," said Sandy, wistfully eyeing Andrea's cheese Danish.

Professor Ross knew Sandy's weakness for pastries. "They're fresh for a change," she said. "Why don't you put that tray down and go get one?"

"I really shouldn't," Sandy murmured, unconsciously smoothing a hip line that seemed to stay perfectly trim no matter what she ate. But she parked her tray on the older woman's table and hurried back over to the service counter.

When she returned, she perched on the edge of a chair while Andrea finished the last few bites and regaled her with a brief synopsis of Sam Jordan's sculpture and Professor Quinn's angry encounter with Mike Szabo.

"Do you think Professor Quinn *is* a thief?" she finished.

Andrea shrugged, not wanting to ruin her digestion with speculations on Riley Quinn's character, and changed the subject. "Who're the extra two cups for?" she asked, gesturing toward the tray.

"Lem and Professor Simpson. Your 'friend' Jake Saxer was around somewhere," she added meaningfully, "but I certainly didn't go looking for him."

She hesitated briefly, as though debating something in her mind, then leaned forward and blurted out, "Look, Andrea, why don't you let me talk to Professor Nauman for you about this Jake Saxer–Professor Quinn business?"

"Absolutely not!"

"But you know how out of it Professor Nauman can be sometimes. He probably hasn't noticed how high-handed Quinn's getting. I know he'd stop it if he realized how unfair it is."

"I mean it, Sandy. I'll fight my own battles with that damn Riley Quinn. You don't have to get involved. Besides," she added as they rose and walked toward the elevator, "you've got enough to worry about. How are David's job prospects looking these days?"

Sandy shook her head, her bright face momentarily dimmed. "He's still just getting the usual form letters: 'We regret to inform you that we anticipate no academic openings in the foreseeable future; however, we *will* keep your letter on file and should circumstances alter . . .'"

"Sounds as though you have the whole routine memorized," Andrea said. She pushed the button to signal the self-service elevator.

"I ought to. I mail out enough of the same sort of letters every week." She tilted her head toward the stack of mail on the tray she carried. "I'll bet at least five of these are job applications. Everyone wants to teach in New York."

"Something's bound to turn up for David," Andrea encouraged.

"Oh, well, if worse comes to worst, I can keep working here after we're married. We could get by on my salary while David finishes his doctorate."

The elevator door opened, and everyone inside exited except a brown-coveralled figure.

"Miss Sandy!" the workman beamed. "Only now I am coming to see you. That chair you want me to fix."

"Oh, that's all right, Mike," Sandy said hastily. "It can wait till next week sometime."

"No, no. I get it today." Armed with the assurance of one who knows himself firmly in the right, Mike Szabo had no hesitation about entering his enemy's domain. He was a stocky man in his late thirties, with dark hair beginning to show gray around the edges of a broad East European face. He took the tray of cups from Sandy's hands with a determined air of rough courtesy.

The elevator stopped for more passengers at each floor until everyone was jammed together, and Sandy, standing in front of Szabo, felt the tray he was holding cut into the back of her thin dress. She hoped all the lids were on tight; she'd hate to walk around all day with a coffee stain across her back.

"Where's Quinn right now?" whispered Andrea in her ear.

"In class for another ten or fifteen minutes if I'm lucky," Sandy whispered back.

It was, in fact, ten-thirty-eight when they parted in the hall: Andrea Ross to pull slides for her eleven-o'clock class on Gothic architecture; Sandy to distribute the hot drinks and ease Mike Szabo out of the area before Quinn came back from his lecture at ten-fifty.

Although the number of staff and students in the Art Department had doubled since open enrollment several years earlier, its original office space atop Van Hoeen Hall had not. Partitioned and repartitioned, that wing of the seventh floor had become a maze of overcrowded, interconnected offices, each shared by at least two (though usually more) staff members. An elevator and stairwell were at the top of the hall opposite a set of rest rooms.

The first office on the right was occupied by several art
historians, including Andrea Ross; the second was mostly
art-studio personnel; and at the end of the hall a third
door opened into two small offices and the slide library,
a tiny room lined with banks of file drawers sized to hold
the two-inch-square glass-mounted slides that were used
to illustrate the survey courses.

There were more than fifty thousand slides in the
collection, yet the historians were always grumbling about
the need for more. "More French impressionists, African
primitives, German cubists! And okay, so we have all of
Picasso's blue period," they might concede, "but what
about his rose period? Practically zilch!"

Only two doors opened on the left side of the hall.
A person could enter the first and turn left again into
the nursery—so called because eight of the most junior
staff members shared the six desks shoehorned into that
narrow office—or veer right into Sandy's office. A two-
sided mail rack with pigeonholes for each departmental
member jutted out into her office. Beyond the mail rack,
doors led into two smaller offices, and a third door gave
onto the hall again.

The decor was late government surplus: nothing
matched. Tables, chairs, desks, file cabinets—almost
everything had been scrounged over the years. Whenever a more favored department got new furnishings,
Piers Leyden's friends in Buildings and Grounds would
let someone from Art salvage such desirable objects as
desks with unbroken drawers, chairs that still swiveled
or better desk lamps. Other offices had carpets and
matching draperies. Art's floor and windows were bare,
and the chairman's telephone was a simple black exten-
sion of Sandy's—there was no way to put someone on
hold, no push buttons to route in extra calls.

All this was not a deliberate shortchanging on Administration's part. Not entirely. By a sort of unspoken
agreement Art balanced its unyielding attitude toward
Administration's officiousness by not clamoring for more
amenities. Most members of the department were happy

to relinquish bigger offices and fancier furnishings in return for their relative independence.

With Mike Szabo trailing her like a shaggy brown dog, Sandy entered this shabby warren of offices by the first door, lifted a cup from the tray he still carried and stepped aside to let the Hungarian pass through to the main office.

"You can just set the tray on the bookcase," she called after him. "The broken chair's that one on the other side of the encyclopedias."

"Hokay," replied Szabo, who'd given Professor Simpson a cheerful salute in passing.

Sandy smiled at the gray-haired professor also and set the cup marked C/W/SUG on his desk in the front corner of the nursery.

Juniors were usually stuck with the early-morning or late-afternoon schedules; they rarely got the desirable midday classes, so the room was empty now except for Professor Simpson. He looked up from a thick tome as Sandy placed his coffee on a desk cluttered by student themes, IBM grade cards, folders and stacks of books with scrap-paper markers fringing their ends.

Albert Simpson had once carried much weight on a large frame. The weight was gone now, and his boniness made him look older, as if he'd shrunk into himself. He seemed to embody the idea of the absentminded professor whose suits were always untidy, whose socks might not match, and who forgot contemporary dates, but who could make dead eras come alive with thousands of intimate details. The elderly classicist had been working on his book about Roman art for almost thirty years, yet it had never progressed beyond the research stage. He kept wandering down too many fascinating side paths ever to organize his mass of findings into a publishable manuscript; but he was David Wade's graduate advisor, and Sandy was fond of him, so she defended him whenever Professor Quinn or Piers Leyden made caustic remarks about eggs that never hatched.

"Is David in this morning?" Simpson asked now,

peering over his glasses at an outdated schedule taped to the wall above his desk. "I've just come across another passage in Maiuri that supports his thesis."

"No, he's taking in that exhibition at the Metropolitan," Sandy said. She made a mental note to replace the three-year-old schedule with a new one, and this time she'd tape it up herself instead of just handing it to him to get lost on his desk again. "He should be in around noon, though."

"Good, good," murmured the old scholar, already reabsorbed in his text. He probably wouldn't think of the coffee again until it was stone-cold, Sandy thought.

She turned and almost collided with Mike Szabo, who now carried a battered wooden armchair over his head. One of the legs had come unglued and was hanging by its stretchers, the result of some too strenuous roughhousing among the teaching fellows and graduate assistants.

"I have it fixed good for this afternoon," Szabo promised, and Sandy smiled her thanks.

Leaving the nursery, she skirted the mail rack and paused by a long, waist-high bookcase beside the chairman's door. It was another castoff—battered looking but sturdy and capacious enough to hold the department's Britannicas, an unabridged dictionary, several art encyclopedias and a dozen or so other reference works. Szabo had left the tray on the end nearer the door to Professor Nauman's office, and Sandy picked up Vance's CHOC and continued on around the corner with it.

Lemuel Vance was a vigorous fifty, with thick black hair only lightly sprinkled with gray. He was more of a technician than an intellectual, but he knew as much as any man living about how to achieve every subtle effect possible in the realm of graphics. He raged, bellowed, cursed, had even been known to deliver a stinging smack to the backsides of his most talented students when they slacked their standards; but he was an effective, respected teacher, and he got results. Over the years many of his former students had carved out quite respectable niches in the art world.

Sandy found the barrel-shaped printer lusting over a glossy catalog of heavy equipment and preparing his annual raid on the department's budget.

"You could type up the requisition order, slip it in with some other stuff, and Oscar'd never notice he'd signed it," Vance said, continuing an earlier argument.

"I still don't see what's wrong with the printing press you have," Sandy smiled.

"Are you kidding? Eighteen inches—that's the biggest plate that antediluvian junk heap can take. Now *this* beauty," he crooned, touching a picture in the catalog with inkstained fingers, "can take plates twice that big."

Sandy studied the description. Most of the technical terms were beyond her. The astronomical price she could understand, though, as well as the machine's gross shipping weight. "Could the floor support that much extra weight?"

"So they have to put jacks under it, so what?" Vance said impatiently, dismissing what would certainly be screams of outrage from Modern Languages directly beneath the printmaking workshop. "Come on, Sandy, help me talk Oscar into it. How can I teach etching without a decent press?"

"Professor Nauman isn't a dictator, Lem. Something this expensive he'd want the whole department to vote on. Anyhow, you know Professor Quinn doesn't feel the historians have been getting their fair share of the budget. Haven't you heard him? He thinks the slide collection should be doubled, and that'll mean new file cabinets and probably remodeling, and there goes this year's budget."

"Those parasites! Without artists where would those damn historians be?" he asked darkly. "Riley Quinn won't be happy till he's bought a slide of every piece of art that's ever been photographed. To hell with buying necessities to teach new artists! You think he cares that I've got kids waiting in line half the period to use a press?"

Vance was still griping at ten-forty-three when Sandy slipped down the hall to wash her hands. Considering the lavatory's location and clientele, the caricatures and graffiti decorating its walls weren't too pornographic. Figure classes increased one's draftsmanship but took a lot of fun and spice out of anatomical nudes. Of course, someone had rather wittily combined Piers Leyden's reputation for romantic dalliance with a well-known Pompeian wall painting of Priapus; and someone else's despairing scrawl "I hate periods!" had been answered by a brisk "Then try semicolons—they're more artistic."

With her mind elsewhere Sandy barely noticed the decorations. She dried her hands and hurried back down the hallway. Professor Simpson didn't look up from his books as she repassed him, and his unopened coffee was still sitting exactly where she had placed it.

Inside her own office she took the cup marked BLK from the tray and set it and the cheese Danish on her desk. The last two cups—both labeled C/W/SUG—she left on the bookcase for Professors Nauman and Quinn, chairman and deputy chairman, who shared the inner office, a preference for sugared coffee and very little else.

As she distributed mail among the pigeonholes of the large rack at the front of the office, a noise drew her attention to a weak-mouthed young man who had appeared behind her by the closed door to the inner office.

"Oh, Harley," she said. "I tried to call you before."

"What about?" the graduate student asked suspiciously. Harley Harris was shorter than she, with petulant eyes and beardless baby-smooth cheeks. He had tried to coax his lank brown hair into an Afro, but it was uncooperative and merely looked messy.

"I called your house three times," Sandy said, "but no one answered. That meeting you wanted with Professor Nauman at eleven—he's scheduled to see the dean of faculties at eleven-fifteen so you'll have to wait till two to meet with him. I'm sorry, Harley."

"Puke on the dean! Let him wait! Or is Nauman afraid to see me? Afraid I'll raise a stink?" His voice rose in a whine. "Listen, Sandy, they're wrecking me. If I don't get that degree, I can't teach; and if I don't teach, when'll I have time to paint?"

Sandy gave an inaudible groan. If Harley Harris were lazy or less dedicated, she thought, echoing departmental sentiment, he could have been deflected from the Master of Fine Arts program long ago; but what could be done with an energetic grind whose mawkish, ill-proportioned, beetle-busy landscapes weren't even good kitsch?

It was Piers Leyden, with his perverted sense of humor and disdain for degrees, who had conned the department into letting Harris into the program; who had insisted Harris had the makings of a primitive artist—another Rousseau or Bombois. Unfortunately Harley Harris wasn't even another Grandma Moses.

The joke had stopped being funny. A graduate, after all, reflects the quality of the institution awarding the degree, and the other faculty members were determined that Harley Harris was not going to reflect on *them*. He had been informed that he would not be receiving an M.F.A. degree next month.

"If I can't teach, I'll have to take a job with my old man," Harley complained.

"Oh, stop whining!" said Sandy, stuffing pigeon-holes angrily. "You're lucky to have your father to fall back on."

The senior Mr. Harris owned a thriving window-dressing business in Brooklyn. He had loved the way Harley could write SPRING FASHION SALE in blue-birds and daisies when the lad was only sixteen, and he didn't think six years of college had improved his son's technique. Most of Vanderlyn's Art Department agreed with him.

"You don't have the foggiest idea of how tight the job market is right now," she added impatiently. "Do you know how many people in this country can't find a job? Not just the job they want, *any* job! And if you think an M.F.A.'s a sure ticket to college teaching, forget it!

Look at David—for the last three months we've papered
the whole country with his curriculum vitae, and he still
hasn't found an opening!"

The murmur of changing classes signaled the end
of the third lecture period. Ten-fifty. Sandy turned and
saw Harley Harris now leaning over the bookcase to glare
at a jewel-toned abstract on the wall above.

"Nauman says *my* work's fuzzy and tasteless—what
the hell does he call this muck?"

Since examples of Oscar Nauman's "muck" hung in
major museums all over the world, Sandy overlooked his
peevish insult.

Suddenly the door of the inner office opened, and
a thin blond man emerged. "Phone calls," he announced
blandly, and Sandy wondered how much he had heard
of her outburst. Jake Saxer was by no means one of her
favorites.

Everything about him was just a little too crisp and
hard-edged. Even his straw-colored beard was precisely
clipped to a Vandyke point. Andrea Ross called him a
Plexiglas construction straight out of minimal art, and
he did have the brittle two-dimensional intensity of a
man who expects to make it before forty. At twenty-
seven Saxer already had his Ph.D. and an assistant professorship. Upon his arrival at Vanderlyn College two
years ago, he'd analyzed his opportunities like a hard-
nosed curator assessing the authenticity of a dubious
Etruscan warrior and then deliberately ingratiated himself with Professor Quinn. Quinn had just begun another
definitive book on postwar trends in modern art, and
Saxer was knowledgeable about sources, references and
illustrations. He had made himself so indispensable
that Quinn had used his authority as deputy chairman
to cut Saxer's teaching load to one survey course this
semester—ostensibly so that Saxer could sort and catalog
the department's chaotic slide library but in reality to
give him more free time for Quinn's research chores.

The office continued to fill up as people drifted in
from classes to check their mail or just shoot the breeze.

Piers Leyden and Andrea Ross were followed by Vance, who came in sipping his hot chocolate. Graduate students and lecturers, holding coffee and cigarettes, elbowed for space at the corner table, gossiping about the morning fiasco in hoots of laughter, which moderated slightly when Riley Quinn returned from his ten-o'clock lecture, "Conceptual Divergence in Modern Art."

All signs of the deputy chairman's earlier loss of control had vanished. Once again he was a supercilious, dapper executive with a tanned face, crisp gray hair and shrewd brown eyes. Quinn always seemed to have just emerged from an expensive barbershop, his nails freshly manicured and trailing a faint scent of after-shave lotion; and in a department not noted for sartorial elegance his perfectly pressed fawn-colored suit, dark brown shirt and paisley tie set him apart. Not a speck of city dust dulled the gleaming surface of his shoes, and his pigskin slide case was custom-made and unbattered.

Harley Harris rose from a chair beside the bookcase. "Professor Quinn—"

"Not now," Quinn said brusquely. "Sandy, get me Dean Ellis." He reached around Harris and picked up one of the two Styrofoam cups on the bookcase.

"Now just a minute!" Harris squeaked. "I have a right—"

Quinn ignored him and, seeing Sandy signal that the dean was on the line, went into his office and closed the door in Harley Harris's face. Harris turned angrily and almost collided with Professor Simpson, who was balancing his coffee on two thick reference tomes.

"Excuse me," murmured the old man and, nudging the boy aside, returned the books to the shelves below. Beyond Simpson's bent back Harris spotted Oscar Nauman just making his way through the crowded office, and his truculence wavered.

White-haired, six-foot-two, and possessed of deep blue eyes that seemed to look past externals to the heart of any matter, the chairman towered over his colleagues mentally as well as physically. He tended to forget appointments and responsibilities, and left most departmental routine to Quinn and Sandy. When aroused in intellectual debate, his speech often became tangled and elliptical because his mind outran his tongue; but in his writings and especially in his paintings his brilliance shone forth unhindered. The only criticism ever leveled at Oscar Nauman's work was that it was too starkly cerebral.

Now he took the last cup from the tray on the bookcase, discarded the snap-on lid, swallowed deeply and grimaced, "God, Vance! This tastes like one of your acid baths!"

All this time Harley Harris, who barely came up to Nauman's chest, had been dancing for attention, and the artist looked down at him in mystified bewilderment as a Great Dane might gaze at a yipping chihuahua. Frustrated, Harris shrilled, "You just wait then! You'll be sorry! And I hope you roast in hell!"

Nauman watched him flounce away through the nursery exit and, honestly puzzled, appealed to Sandy. "Is he upset about something?"

Malicious laughter rippled through the big room as Sandy reminded him of Harley's failure. "Professor Quinn told him yesterday that he wouldn't qualify for an M.F.A., but I think he was hoping you'd override the committee's decision. He was supposed to have a meeting with you today but it had to be postponed."

Nauman frowned, uncomfortably aware that he'd been unintentionally rude to the boy. He could be, and often was, merciless in his treatment of those with intellectual pretensions, but picking on someone of Harley Harris's mental size was not very sporting.

Around him the conversation had reached a raucous pitch. Among the younger staff members at the corner table, battle was joined over whether or not there was a shred of individuality in the whole second generation of abstract expressionists. Both sides had fervent, articulate defenders who shouted to be heard.

A bearded latecomer pushed his way into the group,

snarling good-naturedly at a friend who'd maneuvered him into dating his girl friend's cousin. "You promised me a Venus," he grumbled. "She was a Venus, all right. The Willendorf Venus!"

Which led to fertility symbols, Paleolithic cave paintings, Stonehenge, Toltec technology and present-day earthworks and "—so his uncle's in the business, and he can borrow a bulldozer whenever—"

"I'll be damned if I'll buy it. What kind of art is it if you've got to go up five miles in a frigging helicopter everytime you want to see the whole thing?"

"Ah, you're a reactionary—"

"—combines soft sculpture with collage and gets—"

"—so I told him where he could put holography, and *she* said—"

Nauman shook his head over so much simultaneous vociferous enthusiasm, but on the whole he approved. Some of his best paintings had been generated by free-wheeling debate. He took a final gulp of the really un-palatable coffee and set the empty cup on the file cabinet between two of Sandy's potted geraniums while he pulled out an elaborately carved meerschaum pipe. As he lit it, he was cornered by Lemuel Vance, who began but-tressing his demand for a new printing press for the graphics workshop with data from three different cata-logs. He almost had to shout to be heard over the sur-rounding din.

In the midst of all the loud hilarity and noisy ar-guments Sandy noticed a girl hesitating by the mail rack. At Sandy's gesture the girl, a student aide from Dean Ellis's office, edged her way over. Clearly such bedlam never occurred in the hushed sanctuaries below.

"The dean wants to know if Professor Quinn's all right," she whispered.

"All right?" repeated Sandy in a puzzled tone. The decibel level began dropping as others became aware of this new diversion and paused to eavesdrop.

The girl nodded. "Dean Ellis was speaking with Professor Quinn on the telephone when he suddenly started—I mean, the dean said it sounded like Professor Quinn was—" Embarrassed, she groped for a diplomatic term. "Like he was, well, you know, *upchucking.*"

Sandy half rose. Nauman was closer to the door, but before he could move it was wrenched open and Riley Quinn staggered across the threshold. He clutched a wastebasket to his soiled shirtfront, and an acrid stench reached their nostrils as he heaved into it spasmodically. His eyes were glassy, his skin green-white beneath its deep tan.

"Help me!" he gasped hoarsely, retching at every word. "Oh, my God, I'm dying!"

The ambulance responded in record time, but Quinn had passed into a deep coma before it arrived. Death occurred shortly after twelve noon.

4

Sigrid Harald was not a particularly fervent proponent of the Equal Rights Amendment. She waved no banners, marched in no demonstrations, signed no petitions for the advancement of women. She was aware of how much she owed to the feminist movement, but she also knew the worth of her own brains and stamina, and she had expected to reach her present position on the police force before she was thirty-five; ERA just speeded up the timetable. For that she was grateful; and when promotion to lieutenant and an opening in the Detective Bureau were offered so much earlier than she'd hoped and planned, she had accepted it for what it could be, not for what it was.

"I'm not here to be the department's token female officer," she'd told Captain McKinnon equably. "If you won't give me a share of the case loads just like any other officer—the paperwork *and* the street work—then you'd better get another female."

McKinnon had glared at her. Men he knew how to handle; men could be wilted by a blast of his anger; but women—he'd never commanded women on a regular basis, and this one wasn't easily intimidated. Those cool gray eyes refused to waver.

"You'll take what's assigned, and you'll work by the rules," he'd said. "*My* rules. The commissioner wished you on me, but I'm still running things here. I'll expect the same obedience and respect I get from all my officers, or by damn I *will* get another female!"

She'd nodded. She was a tall, slender woman. Slender almost to the point of skinny; only not skinny in the dried-up sense, thought McKinnon, but fined down

25

like a greyhound or a ballet dancer. Hair as dark as her
mother's had been; tall like her father with his fair Nordic
skin. A self-contained person totally unlike Anne or Leif.
Not at all pretty, yet there was something about those
level gray eyes, something that had made McKinnon
hope she would work out here.

Nearly a year had gone by since then; and when
the call came in from a local precinct station about
a possible poisoning at Vanderlyn College, McKinnon
checked the work sheets and was glad to see that Lieutenant Harald's was the lightest case load at the moment.
The young woman had shown herself capable of handling
violence, but (although he would have denied it) Mac
always breathed easier when he could legitimately give
Anne Harald's daughter what he privately tagged the
"amateur" murders: the single eruption of violence between friends or relatives that usually left a remorseful
killer confessing at the scene of his crime. A homicide
at a college—especially a poisoning—how dangerous could
it be?

Lieutenant Harald was unaware that Captain McKinnon
had once known her parents, and she would have been
indignant if she'd heard his reasoning. When the new
assignment was relayed to her, she was cleaning up
the loose ends of a routine case, a dope-pushing doctor
who'd been knifed when he refused credit to a young
hophead desperate for a quick fix. The dreary incident
had occurred during office hours in front of the doctor's
receptionist and two patients, and the kid had been picked
up a half hour later, so any reasonably competent pros-
ecutor should be able to get a conviction. Always nice
when the current assignment was wrapped up as the
new one began; unfortunately it didn't happen often
enough.

On her way to Vanderlyn College, Lieutenant Harald stopped by the small hospital where Professor Quinn
had died. In a holding area off the emergency room,
Cohen, an assistant from the Medical Examiner's Office,

had finished his superficial examination and was waiting for her before removing Quinn's body for a complete autopsy.

"Offhand I'd say ingestion of some sort of metallic irritant," he said, pulling back the sheet and pointing to the corrosive burns on the dead man's lips. "I'll know better after I open him up."

"How soon?" she asked, trying to match Cohen's dispassionate mood.

He shrugged. "There's a drowning and two suicides ahead of you today, but ladies first, I guess. I'll put yours at the head of the line. Nice threads," he added reflectively, gazing at the no longer immaculate fawn suit and the crumpled and befouled paisley tie which lay across the bottom of the stretcher. "Too bad they got puked on."

He dropped the sheet over Riley Quinn's body again.

Vanderlyn College employed its own security personnel to police the campus, but when Sigrid Harald was still a uniformed rookie, she had ridden a patrol car in this precinct for a few months before being transferred, so she had a working knowledge of the college layout. Except for the river promenade Vanderlyn's tree-graced grounds were completely enclosed by a tall ivy-covered brick wall broken in several places by broad wrought-iron archways with gates that could be locked at night. All legal spaces on both sides of the street for a three-block radius were jammed with cars, motorcycles and mopeds, and several privately owned parking garages on side streets were guaranteed a turn-away business because of the warning signs posted on every gate onto the campus: Official Vehicles Only—Absolutely No Parking on Campus.

Sigrid flashed her shield at a beefy-faced uniformed patrol officer lounging in front of the main gate.

The officer gave her a dour nod and gestured toward a narrow service street to the left, which eventually brought her to the rear of Van Hoeen Hall, where several other police vehicles were parked in a delivery zone. By the time she located the Art Department, it was nearly three-thirty. Personnel from precinct and head-quarters were, as always, overlapping in the prelimi-naries, amiably arguing points of precedence; but the lab technicians seemed to have settled in with their usual efficiency.

Another uniformed officer was posted at the top of the hall by the elevator doors to keep back a crowd of blue-jeaned students who craned their necks and jostled for good sight-seeing positions. Sigrid heard a buzz of curious speculation as she again flashed her shield.

"What do you call a lady pig?" asked an adenoidal voice, but the gibe was good-natured and was even ac-companied by a couple of embarrassed shushes. There had been no demonstrations at Vanderlyn in several years.

She entered the Art Department's main office by way of the nursery door, and her glance brushed over the group of people seated on a motley collection of ill-matched chairs around a long table in the front corner. The office reminded her of those in old precinct stations throughout the city. There were the same unlovely tile floors, a battered bookcase, a large desk canted across a rear corner and under the high windows a bank of ugly green, black and brown file cabinets, some with sprung drawers that would never again close flush.

The resemblance to precinct houses ended there, however, for large bright paintings—mostly abstract—covered the cream-colored walls; baskets of Swedish ivy, asparagus ferns, spider plants and the like hung in front of the windows, and pots of geraniums stood on the file cabinets, softening the room's bureaucratic feel. Someone evidently had a kelly green thumb or amazing luck, thought Sigrid, who'd never managed to keep a plant alive for more than a month and no longer tried.

An assemblage of small white nonrepresentational sculptures, none more than eight inches high, stood on the file cabinets in front of the plants. They had all been carved from blocks of plaster of Paris, and each was intricately detailed with a variety of surface textures. One ambitious piece looked like a random pile of barred cages with small cubes inside. Not very aesthetic perhaps but remarkable when one realized that it had been carved from a solid chunk of plaster. Later Sigrid would learn that these sculptures were not the handiwork of art majors but had come out of a workshop course that the Art Department gave to teach predental students dexterity in using small tools in a confined space.

At the moment, however, most of her attention was focused not on the plaster sculptures atop the file cabinets but on the cherubic-faced man who waited for her in front of them. He carried a folder, and past experience told her it must already hold the rough beginnings of timetables, character sketches, floor plans and anything else that had caught his attention.

"I've made a few notes, Lieutenant," he said anxiously.

Detective Tildon—inevitably rechristened "Tillie the Toiler" by his colleagues—found it very difficult to make comparisons, draw parallels, formulate theories or see beyond the obvious; but to compensate for his lack of imagination, he followed the book to the letter, and he was scrupulous about detail. Tillie's reports were sometimes officialdom's despair, sometimes its salvation. Legend had it that he once used three sheets of paper to describe one ordinary cocktail glass found at the scene of a murder—but the detective in charge wouldn't have thought twice about the triangular-shaped chip of glass embedded in the heel of the murderer's shoe if he hadn't remembered Tillie's sketch of the cocktail glass's missing chip.

Plowing through Detective Tildon's mountains of verbiage could be exasperating; yet, on the whole, Sigrid

approved of his thoroughness. Occasionally he was too
anxious to please, and his feelings were easily hurt, but
Sigrid preferred him to the hotshot macho types who
bordered on insubordination when required to take or-
ders from her.

Now Tillie described the situation to her in low
undertones. He explained his sketch of the department, filled her in on the people he'd talked to so far
and told why he'd detained these particular seven to
wait for her questions. He had listed them in order of
seniority:

Prof. Oscar Nauman, Chairman, Color and Basic
Design

Assoc. Prof. Albert Simpson, History of Classical Art

Assoc. Prof. Lemuel Vance, Advanced Printmaking

Asst. Prof. Piers Leyden, Life Painting

Asst. Prof. Andrea Ross, History of Medieval Art

Asst. Prof. Jake Saxer, History of Modern Art/Slide
Curator

Miss Sandy Keppler, Secretary

No one was better than Detective Tildon in preliminary interviews. Witnesses were so disarmed by his
cheerful, bumbling manner that they often said more
than they'd intended. And Tillie wrote it all down in a
neat, precise script.

Sigrid seated herself at Sandy Keppler's desk and
slowly reviewed his notes. She'd seen the raised eyebrows when Tillie called her by her title and decided
the witnesses could use the extra time to get used to the
idea that a female police officer would be conducting the
investigation. Her height and her no-nonsense appearance helped. At five-ten, her dark hair braided into a
knot at the nape of her neck and wearing a loose, rather
poorly tailored pantsuit, she looked efficient and capable
of command.

At last she lifted her head from Tillie's notes and
spoke in the quiet voice that always warranted attention.
"My name is Lieutenant Harald, and I'll try not to keep

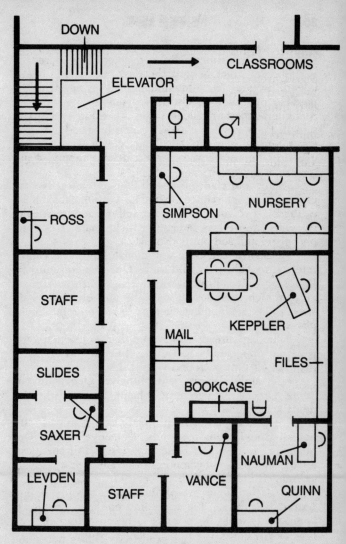

DOWN

CLASSROOMS

ELEVATOR

NURSERY

SIMPSON

ROSS

STAFF

KEPPLER

MAIL

FILES

SLIDES

BOOKCASE

SAXER

NAUMAN

VANCE

LEVDEN

STAFF

QUINN

ART DEPARTMENT OFFICES,
SEVENTH FLOOR,
VAN HOEEN HALL
(Sketch by Detective Tildon)

you any longer than necessary. First, is access to the Chemistry Department very convenient from here?"

She sat erect behind the desk, her hands neatly folded, her gray eyes watchful; and all seven—with the possible exception of Oscar Nauman—were suddenly reminded of certain teachers they'd faced in elementary school. Piers Leyden cheekily raised his hand.

"If it's poisons you're looking for, why go all the way over to Chemistry? We've got a decent supply of our own right downstairs."

"State your choice," agreed Lemuel Vance. He had exchanged his ink-stained lab coat for a disreputable brown cardigan. "I've got nitric, acetic, sulfuric and hydrochloric acids, as well as potassium dichromate, trisodium phosphate and sodium hydroxide."

He had meant to be sensational; but Sigrid calmly referred to Tillie's list and said, "Oh, yes, you must be Professor Vance. Printmaking."

"Which includes lithography and etching," said Vance. "The acids and alkalies are to bite lines into metal plates."

Tillie had already discovered that no teacher could resist an opportunity to lecture, but he was stunned. "You let *kids* mess around with that stuff?"

"Certainly!" Vance said blithely. "One learns by doing, Officer. An eye here, a hand there and the students get cautious."

"Stop being cute, Lem," said Oscar Nauman. "It's not as dangerous as it sounds, Detective Tildon. Our beginners work under close supervision. All chemicals are locked up except when Professor Vance or a graduate assistant is in the workshop."

"It's the same for photography," Sandy volunteered helpfully. "I guess some of those developer compounds must be poisonous because they're kept locked up, too."

"Who has the keys?" asked Sigrid.

"I do," said the girl. "There in the top right drawer."

Sigrid fished them out and handed them to Tillie, who signaled to one of the lab personnel and slipped out to check on the chemical supplies.

"Who knew where the keys were kept?" asked Sigrid.

"Why, practically everybody," Sandy replied. "Seniors and majors are supposed to work independently when classes aren't in session, so they just reach in and take the room key they need. Of course, they're supposed to sign for them; and as Professor Nauman said, they aren't *supposed* to use any chemicals without supervision."

Her tone implied that the rules weren't stringently enforced, and that was confirmed when Sigrid examined the clipboard in the same drawer. It hadn't been signed since the week before.

"I suppose you never lock your desk?"

"Only at night," Sandy admitted unhappily.

Sigrid pulled a fresh sheet of paper toward her. "We'll take it from the top, I think."

There were groans and mutters of fatigue and hunger from her captives—all of whom had missed lunch—but Sigrid ignored them. "Now then, Miss Keppler, when you went downstairs at ten-twenty-five, who else was around?"

More than ever Sandy Keppler was reminded of a third-grade teacher who had stressed precision and accuracy. "Professors Simpson and Vance were the only ones I actually saw," she said carefully.

"Don't be tactful, my child," said a genial Piers Leyden. "You knew Saxer and I were floating around somewhere."

"Okay," said Sandy, tossing back a lock of golden hair. "You both were here, too, but so far as I know, that's all. There were a couple of lecturers who finished at ten, and another graduate assistant was supposed to be here; but she went home at ten, too. Do you want their names?"

"Not at the moment," Sigrid said. She skipped to another name on Tillie's list. "Professor Nauman was in class then, but what about you, Professor Ross?"

Sigrid recognized that she and Andrea Ross were about the same age, but the professor made more concessions to femininity. She wore a well-cut navy pantsuit and a white ruffled shirt, which softened her thin face. Her short brown hair was slightly waved, and there was a porcelain quality about her complexion.

"Did you come upstairs earlier?" Sigrid asked.

"And help myself to poison in time to get back to the snack bar for breakfast before Sandy so obligingly set her tray down on my table? Sorry, Lieutenant. I arrived here *with* the coffee, not before."

Her tone was light, but Sigrid noticed her clenched hands and white knuckles as she toyed with an unopened pack of cigarettes.

"Detective Tildon has given me the gist of Miss Keppler's conversations with Professors Vance and Simpson," she said, "but not with you."

"It wasn't anything!" cried Sandy.

Andrea Ross waved off the young secretary's quick protest. "Never mind, Sandy. I haven't made a secret of my feelings," she said. "Two days ago I learned that Professor Quinn had recommended Jake Saxer for promotion over me. You must have had similar experiences, Lieutenant. How did they make *you* feel?"

When Sigrid didn't answer, Professor Ross shrugged insultingly and ripped the cellophane from the cigarette package. "Or maybe you haven't. Maybe you're the Police Department's showcase model—the one they point to whenever rank-and-file women start complaining that they aren't getting the same breaks as the men."

Sigrid continued to gaze at her with neutral gray eyes, and Andrea Ross flushed. Her own eyes wavered for a moment, and then she said defiantly, "I have a Ph.D., seniority and better evaluations from my students; but I didn't cozy up to Riley Quinn, and I'm not a man, so Saxer gets my promotion. And yes, I'm pretty damn bitter about it. But I didn't slip poison into Quinn's coffee while Sandy had her back turned. Not downstairs and not here!"

She extracted a cigarette, lighted it and inhaled deeply. Saxer's thin lips had tightened at the implied insult, but he remained silent.

"And after you and Miss Keppler returned to this floor?"

"For what it's worth I was in the slide room preparing for my class when the ten-o'clock lectures finished," said Ross. "Professor Leyden was in his office when I first went past, but I'm not sure of the time."

"Wish I could reciprocate," Leyden said fliply, "but I never saw you, kid. My back was to the door, and I just assumed all that in-and-outing was Jake."

"Professor Simpson?"

"I'm sorry," apologized the elderly historian. "I was absorbed in a new book on Herculaneum, but I don't think anyone came past my desk except Miss Keppler. Of course, someone could have entered by the other door, and I wouldn't have seen him. The mail rack completely blocks my view of that door."

"And you were in the inner office alone, Professor Saxer?"

The blond teacher glared at her haughtily. "I had telephone calls to make, Lieutenant. There are only two telephones on this whole floor: the one inside and Sandy's. And you've seen what a crossroads of the western world this outer office is."

"He's right," said Sandy in answer to Sigrid's inquiring gaze. "Everyone phones from the inner office if it's empty. It's more private."

"Anyhow," said Saxer, "Sandy hadn't brought the coffee up before I went inside, and she and that Harris kid were both here when I finished."

"But you *and* the coffee were alone while Sandy was in with me!" Vance chortled. "You could be the winner, Jake!"

Saxer's pale face grew even paler with suppressed

fury, but he managed a tight smile beneath his yellow beard. "And where were *you* when Sandy went tripping down the hall to wash her hands?"

He turned back to Sigrid. "All this talk about who *could* have done it is pointless. Any of us could have—even Sandy—but what about the one person we *know* was hanging over that bookcase? Why aren't you questioning Leyden's protégé?"

"Who's that?" she asked, sorting through Tillie's notes and wondering who was missing.

"Harley Harris, that's who!"

"You gotta be kidding," said Vance. "That kid's too incompetent to be a poisoner. You ever see him open a tube of paint?"

Sigrid's faith in Tillie was restored as she found his comments on the absent graduate student, his last peevish remarks and his failure. She read through them briefly and squelched Vance's impromptu imitation of the boy by saying, "We'll certainly want to talk with him, but in the meantime—"

"As long as you're on who's missing, there's someone else," observed Andrea Ross. "That Mike What's-his-name, Karoly's nephew."

"Mike Szabo?" asked Leyden. "That was a lot earlier, wasn't it? And downstairs. Mike wasn't—"

"Yes, he was," Sandy interrupted. "He came up on the elevator with Andrea and me to get that chair Phil and Jaime broke last week."

"He even carried the tray," Andrea reminded her. "Remember when it got so crowded? We had our back to him for the last three floors."

"Could he have put something in a cup with just one hand?" Sandy asked. "Anyhow, how would he have known which was Professor Quinn's cup? There were four coffees and Lem's hot chocolate."

Professor Simpson cleared his throat. "Didn't he carry the tray into your office alone?"

"Mike wouldn't have poisoned Riley," Leyden objected. "Hit him over the head with a baseball bat, yes; nag him to death, yes; but poison?"

"Who is Mike Szabo?" asked Sigrid, knowing this must be their first mention of the man as a possible suspect since his name did not appear in Tillie's notes.

Several started to answer, but Oscar Nauman's deep voice carried. "He's a Hungarian refugee employed by Buildings and Grounds and the son of Janos Karoly's only sister."

It was clear the name meant nothing to Sigrid.

"Janos Karoly was an abstract artist who came to prominence here in the fifties, Lieutenant," explained Jake Saxer, the hint of a sneer in his voice, implying he thought her an ignorant philistine. "He died in the early sixties and left all his paintings to Riley Quinn. His reputation is still growing, and the paintings become more valuable every year. Mike Szabo thinks they should have gone to him—he was still in Hungary at the time, hadn't corresponded with Karoly or anything in his whole life, but he still thought Professor Quinn somehow cheated him out of an inheritance."

"Did he?" asked Sigrid.

"Of course not! It was all perfectly legal."

"Yeah? Then why wouldn't Riley let Mike see Karoly's notebooks?" asked Leyden.

"Why should he?"

"The question is, why shouldn't he?" gibed the neo-realist. "Riley could read Karoly's French, but I'll bet you two wooden nickels and a pug dog he was afraid of what those Hungarian passages had in them. We've all heard about how he covered those up whenever he let anyone look at the notebooks."

Saxer shrugged. "I wouldn't know. I don't read Hungarian."

"Neither did anyone else in Riley's pocket," taunted Leyden. "That's why he was afraid to let Mike see them."

"That illiterate peasant! Do you think he cares about

his uncle's genius? All he wants with the paintings is the money."

"And what the hell did Quinn want?" chimed in Lemuel Vance. "The way he kept pushing up Karoly's reputation with those articles in *The Loaded Brush* and *Arts Today*. You think that didn't jack up the price every time he put one of the paintings on the market?"

Jake Saxer bit off a sharp retort as all three men suddenly remembered why Sigrid was following their exchange so intently. They subsided with sheepish faces.

"Thank you, gentlemen," she said dryly and turned to Sandy again. "To recapitulate: this Mike Szabo, who seems to have had a grudge against Professor Quinn, carried in the tray for you and was alone with it for a few minutes?"

"Well, yes," said Sandy, "but really he barely had time to set it down and pick up the broken chair before he was back out again."

"And am I correct in assuming that you always left two cups, with sugar clearly marked, in a tray on that bookcase every morning?"

"Just Monday, Wednesday and Friday. Professor Nauman isn't here on Tuesdays and Thursdays, and Professor Quinn has—*had*—third period free then, so I'd just take it on in to him at his desk those two days."

"But the two cups would be there by ten-forty the other three days?"

Sandy nodded. "By ten-forty-five, anyhow. I got back a little early today."

"Wait a minute!" cried Vance, springing up from his chair and rushing over to the bookcase. "There were *two* cups sitting here, both exactly alike, right? So how could anyone be sure which one Riley would take?"

"Congratulations for finally seeing the obvious," Leyden said sourly. "Better hire yourself an official taster till they catch him, Oscar."

"Is that a suggestion or a warning?" asked the white-haired chairman with a half smile.

"What about it, Miss Keppler?" asked Sigrid. "Was there a pattern as to who took which cup?"

The girl seemed genuinely puzzled. "I'm not sure. Professor Quinn lectured just down the hall while Professor Nauman's class is on the next floor, so most times Professor Quinn had first choice; but I've never noticed which cup he usually took."

"No? Still, I think we must assume *someone* did," said Sigrid, "unless it didn't make any difference to the murderer. A rather unlikely proposition."

As the implications of her statement sank in, Piers Leyden shook his dark head. "Much as it pains me, I have to say Harley Harris is probably the only one dumb enough to poison a cup of coffee without caring whether Riley or Oscar drank it."

There were quick murmurs of agreement. Someone repeated Harris's threats; another described his anger and frustration at not receiving his master's degree.

"No!"

Oscar Nauman had listened without comments as his eager colleagues heaped blame on the unfortunate Harris, and now he cut across their accusations, silencing them. "Rotten taste," he said firmly, "but all the time, and anyhow no one liked him."

Obviously he thought his statement made the graduate student's innocence crystal clear. Sigrid looked blank and Lemuel Vance grinned.

"Don't mind him, Lieutenant Harald; Oscar tends to leave out whole paragraphs when he's being logical."

Patiently Nauman elucidated. "Harris is an ant. Constant toil. A drudge. He doesn't socialize. Never comes up for coffee breaks. He's dull witted but just bright enough to know when he's the butt; so he stays downstairs painting all the time. Can't have been up here for coffee more than once or twice in the last year."

Sigrid saw his logic. "So you think he wouldn't have known Miss Keppler's routine with the coffee cups?"

"Precisely," said Nauman. "And the same reservation applies to Mike Szabo."

Sigrid glanced around the circle of attentive faces, but no one seemed inclined to dispute Nauman's observations. She nodded, made a brief notation on her note pad, then gathered up all the papers and neatly aligned their edges. "It will probably be necessary to speak to you again, but that'll be all for now, I think," she said, rising from Sandy's desk and motioning to Detective Tildon, who had reappeared in the doorway during Nauman's statement.

"Class dismissed!" said Leyden, but no one smiled.

The professors drifted away from the office, and Sandy Keppler reclaimed her desk as Sigrid and Tillie conferred with the remaining lab technician, who was awaiting permission to leave. The others had finished with the inner office and already departed.

A young man in wire-rimmed glasses, chinos, and a rumpled shirt had talked his way past the officer at the end of the hall and now stepped around the mail rack. Sigrid saw the blond secretary's face soften at the sight of him.

"David!"

"Hey, you okay?" he asked anxiously.

Her desk was between them, and they didn't actually touch, but Sigrid suddenly felt that she and Tillie and Yanitelli were interlopers. Intimacy always embarrassed her.

She cleared her throat and said, "One thing more, Miss Keppler. Could you type a list of everyone else in the room before Professor Quinn actually went into his office, and put a check by the name of any you remember seeing near the bookcase?"

The girl seemed to pull herself away from another world to focus on Sigrid's request; then she quickly typed the names of teaching fellows, lecturers and graduate students while David Wade lounged against the corner of her desk, watchful and protective.

Sigrid turned back to the remaining lab man. "That'll be all for now, Yanitelli, thanks. On your way out tell that officer at the elevator to check out Buildings and Grounds and see if he can locate a Mike Szabo."

Yanitelli gave a half salute and gratefully departed.

"Did you turn up anything downstairs?" Sigrid asked Tillie beneath the clack of Sandy's typewriter.

"Yes, indeed," said Detective Tildon happily. "I think I've found our poison."

5

Back in his office around the corner Lemuel Vance sat at his desk with his catalogs opened to the coveted printing presses. With Quinn dead, who would inherit the position of deputy chairman? Simpson? Probably. He was the most senior. A pedant, old Bert Simpson, always pottering after obscure details of Roman sculpture, compiling cross-references on the details of toga draping as if it mattered a tinker's damn which shoulder of a statue was left uncovered. But at least he had a proper respect for studio artists, something that pompous, parasitical Riley Quinn'd never had. He never lost sight of the fact that there wouldn't be any classical art if there hadn't been a lot of classical artists first. And he cared about the students, was always there to give them extra help. Too bad so few kids specialized in his area. Yes, Simpson could be led to see that a new press was more important than an enlarged slide library.

In the next office but one, Piers Leyden was calm in his newly acquired power as a less poised Jake Saxer followed him in and closed the door.

Saxer pulled out a briar pipe he'd recently affected and tried to seem casual as he went through the business of filling and lighting it, but his pale eyes, nervous and darting, kept flicking back to the older man apprehensively.

Around the department Piers Leyden was known as a lazy, cynical slob. He was a good-looking sensualist who ate too much, drank too much and spent too much time in too many different beds. At forty the effects hadn't quite begun to show; but hangovers were starting to take a little longer to go away in the mornings, his belt felt a bit tight all the time, and he knew he should be spending more hours in front of his easel. Tachs, his gallery owner, had been somewhat caustic about those last two nudes; he had implied that Leyden was coasting, that maybe Riley Quinn had a point.

Leyden knew why Jake Saxer had followed him, and he didn't intend to make it any easier for the sneaky, whey-faced opportunist.

A small cloud of blue sulfur drifted over to him as Saxer struggled through several kitchen matches trying to get the pipe going. At last he managed two or three jerky puffs. Unfortunately he'd chosen an oversweet blend that smelled more like apple pie than masculine tobacco; still the steady ribbon of smoke seemed to give Saxer confidence.

"A terrible thing, Riley's death," he said.

"Isn't it?" Leyden agreed blandly. "Poor Doris will no doubt be heartbroken. I wonder if anyone's thought to tell her yet?"

Saxer grasped at the opening offered by Doris Quinn's name. "You and Riley may have had your differences, Leyden, but I didn't agree with him on *everything*." He paused significantly, exuding a casual air as he puffed on the pipe. "I know how much Doris respects your judgment—"

He paused again, and Leyden kept his face carefully blank. Inside he was chortling. When he'd first climbed into Doris Quinn's bed, it was to sting Riley; but that smug bastard acted as if their affair only confirmed Quinn's original low opinion of the artist's taste. And now that lusty little wench was going to ensure his place in history. What marvelous irony!

He regarded Jake Saxer as a spider might regard a particularly tasty summer midge and gave the blond historian a wicked smile. "Why, yes, I think Doris would listen to me . . . under the right circumstances, of course."

* * *

Andrea Ross noted the closed door on her way through to the slide room. Losing Quinn's patronage would put Jake Saxer right back among the hoi polloi, she thought, mechanically refiling the slides of Chartres Cathedral that she'd pulled earlier that day. If Simpson became deputy chairman, he'd be promoted to full professor, opening up another associate professorship; and this time, Andrea vowed to herself, viciously slamming shut the last file drawer, she wouldn't sit quietly by while it was handed to a less qualified man!

"Idaho?" Sandy Keppler was incredulous. "There's no such place!"

David Wade grinned at her ruefully through his wire-rimmed glasses. "Yes, Virginia, there *is* an America west of the Hudson River. Contrary to popular belief, there's a whole continent beyond Staten Island. I even have the letter to prove it."

There was still a boyish air about the thin, very young man perched on the front of her desk, but underneath his relaxed banter one could discern a scholarly maturity. He flourished a postmarked envelope in front of Sandy's disbelieving blue eyes.

"But Idaho?" She tasted the name again. "All I can remember from fourth-grade geography lessons is potatoes." She looked at him with city horror. "You're not getting any back-to-the-land ideas, are you?"

"Idiot child! Can you see either of us on a farm? Don't worry, it won't be for long. As soon as I finish my doctorate, we'll make it back to New York."

Sandy continued to look doubtful, unconsciously twisting a long strand of her blond hair. It was a mannerism left over from childhood that David found utterly entrancing.

"I don't know, David. How can you finish your thesis out there without New York's libraries and museums? Once you're out—do you know how many applications this department gets every month? And it's not just here at Vanderlyn. Every academic opening in this city must have at least five hundred Ph.D.'s lined up for it. Oh, damn! If only your contract could be renewed!"

He leaned over and ruffled her hair tenderly. "It'll work out. Trust me. Idaho might be fun. And it sure beats starving. Have you told Nauman you're leaving yet?"

"There's no rush," she hedged. "He knows about us, but I don't want to hand in my resignation downstairs until we're sure you can't find something here. There're lots of applications for my job, too, you know. Oh, David, do we *have* to leave? We could live on my salary without much scrimping—just till you finish your degree and—"

"No way!" David said stubbornly. "I'm not having you slaving to support me—even if we are going to be married."

He took away the severity of his half-serious admonition by bending to kiss her lips gently.

As he turned to go, Sandy asked, "How was the exhibition?"

"I skipped it. Spent the morning at the library instead."

"Downtown?"

"No, here. There were some references I had to recheck. See you at six?"

The girl nodded, trying to push down a small stab of fear. In the next moment David had rounded the corner, and she heard him stop and speak to Professor Simpson before he was hailed by a younger voice and moved out of range down the hall.

A few minutes later the door to the inner office opened, and Oscar Nauman's high-domed head appeared. "I thought David was still here."

"He just left. Want me to try to catch him?"

"No," he said, "it can wait. Has he landed anything yet?"

"Well, there's a college out in Idaho that needs an art teacher."

"*Idaho?*"

"Yeah, me, too." Sandy smiled wistfully. She picked up her steno pad and a sheaf of papers. "There are a few things you *have* to tell me about today. And these letters need a signature."

Nauman groaned. "I was on my way to see Doris Quinn."

"These won't take long," the girl said firmly.

"Sometimes you're too damned efficient," the artist grumbled, but he followed her docilely back into his office.

At his desk at the front of the nursery around the corner Professor Albert Simpson shook his head in private disagreement. He could remember a long string of indifferent civil-servant-type secretaries over the years: a few had been much too fastidious over matters of detail and protocol; the rest inexcusably lazy. Sandy Keppler was the first to combine competence with tolerance.

A sudden thought struck him: if Sandy left, and he were promoted to Quinn's position, he would have to help train a new secretary. Oh, dear! So inconvenient and time-wasting. There had to be some way to keep young Wade on the staff. Silly rules that said a lecturer's contract couldn't be renewed unless he were offered tenure!

As usual Professor Simpson had taken advantage of the acoustics, which channeled all conversation in the outer office right to his desk. He was a shameless eavesdropper once voices penetrated his thoughts, and he had followed the young romance with more than sentimental interest. Those two would be wasted in Idaho. Especially David. The boy had the makings of a brilliant classical scholar. Look at how he'd organized those long-neglected notes on Praxiteles, drawing paralles to Apollonius of Athens, which he, Simpson, had never noticed before.

He'd even toyed with the idea of taking David with him to Pompeii and Herculaneum on his next sabbatical. Let the boy see Western civilization's loftiest expressions of artistic creativity on their native soil. Well, maybe he still would. What else did he have to spend his salary on? Sandy, too. Indeed, why not? David would hardly want to leave his bride behind, and besides, she was an accurate typist; her skills would be useful when he and David started rewriting the book.

Professor Simpson leaned back in his chair and contemplated his dream of the finished book—a vindication of the strength and beauty of works that had stood the test of centuries, a noble creation worth the lifetime he'd lavished on it; quite unlike the here-today-gone-tomorrow ephemera Riley Quinn had wasted so much of the department's money and energies on.

De mortuis nil nisi bonum, he reminded himself. And come to think of it, Lucretius, too, had said something about not speaking ill of the dead, hadn't he?

The elderly classicist's knobbed and veined hands wandered among the piles of books before him as he began a vague search for that Lucretius reference. Very pertinent, as he recalled. . .

Lieutenant Harald and Detective Tildon emerged on the floor below to find it apparently deserted. Tillie had promised to show his superior the probable poison, but he was incapable of ignoring any details that might later prove important. Gravely Sigrid took an interest in what he had to show her along the route that led to their goal.

"These first rooms are small studios for student painters," Detective Tildon explained, referring to his notes as he trotted along beside Sigrid's tall figure. "Harley Harris uses one of them. There're three here and four more scattered around campus. A lot of the classes seem to be held in odd places. The photography lab's in an annex of the library, and somebody said something about a ceramics workshop over at the gym. In what used to be the basketball team's dressing room?"

He looked at his notes doubtfully; his previous academic experience had been limited to night courses at John Jay College of Criminal Justice. But Sigrid nodded, remembering a college roommate who'd complained about

taking a drawing class in the basement of the biology
building. It had reeked of formaldehyde, and so did her
roommate after every session of that class. Art departments seemed to follow a pattern. Redheaded stepchil-
dren, all.

"As soon as Yanitelli tested for fingerprints and got
all the chemical samples he wanted here, we went across
to the library annex and checked out the photography
lab," said Tillie. "There were only a couple of boxes
marked Poison, and Yanitelli doesn't think any of them
fit the bill. He says that developing chemicals used to
come separately and a few were pretty strong—I forget
their names. Anyhow, the only developers and fixatives
that we found were prepared compounds. Yanitelli took
samples, but he said it'd take a lot of the stuff to kill,
diluted like that—more than you could dissolve in one
cup of coffee anyhow."

(What Yanitelli, who had little respect for the academic mind, had actually said was: "It'd take a damned
absentminded egghead not to notice there was a hell of
a lot more powder than coffee in a cup that little." But
Tillie saw no point in repeating that opinion to Lieutenant Harald. It was still not definitely established that she
had a sense of humor.)

They moved along the deserted hallway.

"This next is a lecture room for art historians," said
Tillie.

Sigrid paused to read a schedule tacked to the door.
Professors Saxer, Simpson and Ross were listed as using
the room this semester; in fact, it was where Andrea Ross
had been due to lecture at eleven that morning.

"And here, right across the hall," Tillie said meaningfully, "is the printmaking workshop."

The door was unlocked, and they stepped into a big
boxy studio that smelled of ink and a vaguely metallic,
acrid odor. The opposite wall was all tall windows facing
north, and the space beneath was lined with open shelves
that held an assortment of copper, zinc and aluminum
plates, lithography stones, and drying prints. Makeshift

clotheslines strung across a corner had more prints clipped to them. There were mismatched worktables and stools, and a large hand-operated, antiquated-looking press stood in the center of the room. To Sigrid's untrained eyes it looked like something Ben Franklin might have been right at home with. No wonder Vance complained. A smaller iron press was bolted to one end of a heavy workbench, and a second workbench held two electric hot plates.

Tillie had collared a student earlier for a crash course in the mechanics of printmaking and was eager to share his new knowledge.

"As I understand it, you start with one of those flat zinc or copper plates. If you're going to engrave it, you just gouge out your picture with a steel needle—it's called a burin—and then put ink on it and run it through the printing press. But for an etching, you heat some varnish on the hot plate, coat your plate, and when it cools, you draw your picture by scratching away the varnish. Etching's supposed to be easier than engraving because varnish is softer to get through than the metal. Then you stick it in an acid bath back there."

Along the rear wall were three deep stone sinks connected by stained and pitted counters, which held large shallow plastic trays.

"You mix the chemicals in those trays, stick your plate in, and the acid will eat out the lines you drew without touching the part that still has varnish on it. When you've got the line as deep as you want, you rinse it off, heat the plate again until the varnish is melted, and you can wipe every bit of it off. Then you ink the plate and print it just like you did with the engraving."

"Very concise," said Sigrid and the detective beamed. "Is that the chemical closet over there?"

"Right, ma'am. You can go in. Yanitelli checked for prints and took a sample of everything he thought Quinn could have been poisoned with."

The chemical closet was actually a small supply room lined with shelves that held neat stacks of paper sorted by size and thickness, and cartons and tins of powdered varnish, talc and inks of various colors. Sigrid's eye was drawn to a collection of containers ominously decorated with skulls and crossbones.

"I made a complete inventory," said Detective Tildon, thumping his clipboard.

"And which do you favor?"

"I guess any of them would do it," Tillie said judiciously. "The nitric acid or the sulfuric; but my money's on the end one, the potassium dichromate. That lid was put back crooked, and Yanitelli wasn't the one who spilled some on the shelf. That was already there. And another thing: it was the only one that didn't have any fingerprints at all. That's always significant to me. Remember that cup we found polished clean in that model's kitchen cabinet?"

"No," smiled Sigrid. "That was just before I came, but I remember Captain McKinnon telling me about it. That cup changed a tentative suicide verdict to murder, didn't it?"

"Well, it just stood to reason," said Tillie modestly. "Just like now. One squeaky-clean jar on a shelf full of dusty ones? Uh-uh. Anyhow, the kid I was talking to said their normal procedure was to take all the jars over to the mixing trays and measure the stuff out there, so nothing should have been spilled in here, right?"

The suspect jar seemed to hold orange salt. Underneath the label Potassium Dichromate with the ubiquitous skull and crossbones. Some sophomoric wit had inked a red Marcel Duchamp mustache on the skeletal head and closed one eye socket in a raffish wink.

"I'd like to speak to Professor Vance again," Sigrid said thoughtfully. "See if he's still around, would you, Tillie?"

While she waited for his return, Sigrid walked down the hall to examine the last two classrooms on that floor. They were duplicates of the print workshop in size and north lighting, but the first reeked of turpentine and oil paints and held an undergrowth of various-sized easels.

Canvases in different stages of completion showed a nude girl poised on a stool, one leg outstretched. The neophyte artists were evidently troubled by that leg, for several showed signs of paint build-up there. Charcoal sketches of other nudes, both male and female, were thumbtacked to the molding all around the studio, and the card on the door confirmed that this was indeed Professor Leyden's life class.

The last studio—Prof. Oscar Nauman, Color and Basic Design, read the card on the door—was different again. Despite the bursts of color blocks and circles tacked to the molding, there was a feeling of order, calm and discipline that had been lacking in the first two studios. Drawing tables stood in neat rows, their precision marred only by their tops being tilted at different angles. Twenty-three of the tables were completely bare; the twenty-fourth was littered with a drift of two-inch paper squares in every conceivable shade of red.

A young girl whose hands and face carried smudges of the same reds looked up as Sigrid entered the room and gave her an electric smile. "I did it!" she said, dazed triumph in her voice. "I really did it!"

"Did what?"

"Went from dark red to light pink in nine equal steps. See?"

On the table in front of the girl was a white sheet of paper on which were aligned nine of the little squares of red tones. The gradations shaded from almost black to light pink and reminded Sigrid of a paint store's sample card.

"Is that so very difficult?" asked Sigrid.

"*Difficult!*" the girl hooted. "Boy, it's plain *you* never took Oscar Nauman's color class! What time is it? *Five?* God! No wonder I'm feeling so empty—I've been down here working on this thing since eleven this morning. It's really a hairy problem," she explained. "See, the assignment was to go from dark to light, any color, in nine equal steps."

Sigrid looked puzzled, so the girl tried again. "Look,

I started with this dark red square, right? So dark it's almost black. Then I put down another square that's a little more of a clear red, right?"

Sigrid nodded.

"Now let's say I next tried one of these that's even lighter from further down at the pink end. I'm still going from dark to light, but the difference between this second and third shade is greater than that between the *first* and second. See? It's got to step down exactly equal."

Again Sigrid nodded. "But it still doesn't sound very difficult."

"Want to try? Be my guest," said the girl, pushing all the extra little squares toward Sigrid. "I must have mixed a hundred and fifty different shades."

Intrigued, Sigrid began lining them up as the girl pasted her own final combination on the white paper.

"There," she said after a few moments.

The girl examined Sigrid's maiden effort and shook her head kindly. "Not bad for a first time, but the change is too great between your third and fourth, and you've only used seven shades. Nine's the magic number, no more, no less. Seven's easy and twelve's a snap. Nine's the bastard."

While the girl cleaned her brushes and put away her tools, Sigrid idly shifted the squares. "I had no idea you could spend a whole semester on just color," she mused.

"A semester? You could study it for *years*," the girl assured her, "and still not learn half the stuff Professor Nauman knows about it. Which is weird if you think about it. I mean, look in the school catalog. Everybody else has a string of letters after their names—M.F.A.'s, Ph.D.'s. Nauman has nothing. I heard he didn't even finish high school."

"But he's a good teacher?"

"The best if you're serious about learning rock-bottom, basic fundamentals. Some of the staff, their stuff's based on sneaky little tricks of technique, see? So they're stingy about what they'll share when they're teaching.

Afraid you'll steal it. But Nauman's generous. He'll give you everything he has because *his* work's built on solid truth. If you *could* imitate it, you wouldn't want to because you'd know enough to have your own perception of truth, see?"

"Professor Nauman must be very popular," Sigrid said, recognizing an enthusiast.

"Nope! No way. Lots of people hate his guts," said the girl cheerfully. "Students *and* staff. He gets impatient with stupidity and laziness, and there's lots of both floating around. They're afraid of him. The man's brilliant, see? And sometimes he forgets the rest of us aren't and says what's on his mind without even realizing that he's cutting everybody to splinters. Hey, you through playing with those?" she finished, ready to sweep the superfluous squares of red tones into a wastebasket.

"You're going to throw them away? After all the time you spent making them?"

"Sure! I've got the nine I need. Hey, do you want them? Take them," she said magnanimously. "They'll drive you crazy, but it really is a good exercise for training your color sense."

"Thank you," Sigrid said formally. She collected solitaire games, and this one seemed more engrossing than many.

The girl unearthed a manila envelope, which she filled with the color squares and gave to Sigrid before carefully carrying away her completed project. "I'm going to leave it on Nauman's desk," she said proudly. "He didn't think any of us could do it in less than three days. See you!"

With a friendly wave of her hand the girl was gone, still unaware that murder had occurred overhead while she wrestled with color.

Sigrid followed more slowly. If a student's casual assessment meant anything, it would be a mistake to ignore the possibility that the poisoned coffee might have been meant for Nauman instead of Riley Quinn. Jealousy and resentment could be potent corrosives.

"Oh, there you are, Lieutenant," said Detective Tildon from the doorway of the print workshop. With him was the uniformed officer who'd been sent to collect Mike Szabo. An earnest young rookie, he looked somewhat abashed at having to report failure.

"Sorry, ma'am," he said, "but they told me Szabo took off as soon as he heard about the murder. Not a word to anybody—just up and went, though he was supposed to work till seven tonight. I did get his home address for Detective Tildon."

Tillie touched his clipboard in affirmation that Szabo's address was officially noted.

Sigrid inclined her head. "Very good, Officer. Thank you."

"You still want someone posted upstairs?" he asked.

"No, it's no longer necessary," Sigrid replied. The rookie nodded and left.

"Is this going to take very long?" Lemuel Vance complained as Sigrid and Tillie joined him inside the studio. "I've got a class meeting here at six, and I haven't eaten since breakfast."

"Class?" asked Sigrid. "I thought all classes were canceled for the rest of the day."

"Only for the day people in the department," he said bitterly. "Administration's decreed that since the Continuing Ed. students had no contact with Quinn, canceling classes out of respect for his memory would be, quote, meaningless, unquote. They're ignoring the fact that everyone who teaches at night was Quinn's colleague."

In light of his earlier calm over Quinn's death Sigrid interpreted his present mood as resentment at not getting a night off, and she directed his attention to the supply closet where the chemicals were housed.

"If the stuff that killed Riley really did come from here, maybe we'd better cancel my etching class anyhow. Admin. couldn't object if you told them you don't want

things disturbed," Vance said hopefully, looking around
the small room.

"That won't be necessary," Sigrid said coldly, crushing his plans for an early getaway. "Everything's been
photographed and examined for fingerprints. Tell me,
Professor Vance, what is potassium dichromate used for?"

"You think that's what Riley got?" Lemuel Vance's
eyes followed hers to the red-mustachioed jar. "It's for
etching aluminum plates. Mostly we use copper or zinc,
but I like the kids to know how to do it all. Or at least
be familiar with the techniques. Funny," he said slowly,
"I just ordered a fresh batch last month. The first in—
hell, must be nearly five years."

"Oh?"

"Yeah. Like I said, we don't use much aluminum.
As you can tell, that jar's an old one. I just dumped the
new stuff in on top. But it was delivered to the office
upstairs. I remember Sandy reading off all the warnings
out loud. Jesus! Now I remember Riley saying it sounded
like something the cafeteria could use to jazz up the
soup!"

"Who else was there?" Sigrid asked sharply.

Vance shrugged. "I don't know. The usual crowd,
I suppose."

"Ross, Saxer, Leyden?"

Vance nodded.

"Harris, Simpson . . . or Szabo?"

"No. Szabo comes up to talk to Leyden once in a
while, but that's usually in Leyden's office, not out with
the rest of us in Sandy's office." Vance's brow furrowed
in deeper concentration. "I don't remember Bert Simpson. Harris? No—Oscar was right about him not coming
up much. Who else? David Wade definitely wasn't because he always sits on the corner of Sandy's desk, and
that's where Jake Saxer was leaning to read off the an-
tidote. Not that you're interested in Wade, I guess, but
he's usually up there every break. Young love in bloom,
you know.

"Oscar was there, too. He told me to be sure and warn the kids again about how dangerous these chemicals can be. As if I don't read them the riot act every time they touch the knob of this closet door!"

Remembering his facetious remarks earlier about "an eye here, a hand there," Sigrid was bemused by his indignation.

"One final thing, Professor Vance. Hypothetically speaking, how unusual would it look if a teacher or student or any unauthorized person entered this closet?"

"Hypothetically, not unusual at all if they had the keys," Vance answered with a resurgence of his former cheerfulness. "Especially during the morning hours. The hall door's never locked, and this room is usually empty up until noon every day."

"But wouldn't a student think it strange to see a historian, for instance, entering your workshop when you're not here?"

Vance laughed outright. "Are you kidding? Ninety-five per cent of our students wouldn't think an elephant in chartreuse tights was strange unless it squirted them in the teeth and whistled three bars of 'Yankee Doodle.' You're talking about kids with eyes that see not, neither do they hear. Or if they do, they won't admit it. They'll print a plate with fuzzy lines and swear it looks as crisp as a photo to them. You think you've got 'em to the point where they'll start to observe, and the next thing you know. . ."

But Sigrid, recognizing an ancient grievance, signaled to Tillie and quietly withdrew.

6

Of all New York's native children few were probably less aware of nature's variety than Lieutenant Sigrid Harald. "A primrose by a river's brim" was just another flower to that austere young woman. If pushed, she might be able to distinguish gardenias from chrysanthemums; but she was unlikely to speculate about a tiny yellow flower's cosmic significance unless it turned up clutched in a murder victim's hand.

Others might mark the changing seasons by leaf and blade, by bird song or shifting constellations. Sigrid seldom noticed spring until it became too hot for bulky sweaters, tweed suits and fleece-lined boots; she awoke to summer's passing when she found herself shivering in thin cottons and polyesters. Winter or summer, her clothes were uniformly dark and unadorned, mostly loose-fitting pantsuits chosen for comfort and utility, not style—and certainly not to celebrate the quickening spring days.

Even a drive through Central Park, as on this evening in mid-April, was merely a way of getting from the East to the West side and was not an occasion to admire Manhattan's largest parcel of nature. Ever since sending Detective Tildon home to wife and dinner earlier, Sigrid had been preoccupied with the puzzle of how Riley Quinn's murderer had known he would take the right cup—always assuming, of course, that it had really been meant for Quinn.

Neither the banks of forsythia and azaleas along the curving road nor the masses of spring bulbs now blooming for the pleasure of jaundiced city eyes made any impression on her. She was unconcerned that the oaks and maples that lined the curbs and nearly met over her car were fully leafed out; was oblivious to the vernal softness in the cool night air as she parked her car almost in front of the dead man's brownstone just around the corner from Central Park West in the west seventies.

Six broad shallow steps flanked by pierced stone balustrades led directly up from the sidewalk to a wide door of gleaming varnished oak adorned by a brass knocker and doorknob polished to golden brightness. The front windows seemed to wear their original glass, leaded and beveled, behind a filigree of wrought-iron bars, that were both decorative and practical in a city with such a high burglary rate.

Sigrid knew this type of house well. Her father's aunts and uncles had owned similar houses in Brooklyn near Prospect Park, and as a small child, she had been taken there for visits. She still remembered the high-ceilinged rooms; the dark parquet floors covered with Turkey red carpets; the peacock feathers in tall vases; and Aunt Kirsten's long, lace-covered table, spread with an incredible assortment of strange-tasting food. After tea Uncle Lars would take her over to the Prospect Park zoo to feed the polar bears while Anne, her mother, southern born and bred and therefore doubly alien, remained behind with the aunts, bridging conversational chasms with her high, light chatter. Family ties were very important to Anne, who for Sigrid's sake had kept up with her dead husband's people. The aunts and uncles in their turn had pitied the plain, gawky child Sigrid had been and always included her in family gatherings. Over the years these had gradually dwindled as the oldest generation died out. The connection with her father's cousins was tenuous by the time Sigrid reached maturity, but she had never forgotten those long-ago Sunday afternoons and those tall spacious houses.

Nowadays such houses were at a premium again, especially in this part of Manhattan. The new owners either restored them to their former elegance, all dark wood and understated antiques, or else gutted the insides, lowered ceilings and created dramatically modern interiors behind the old facades. In any event, there would be a small, exquisite garden in the rear, just large enough for smart cocktail parties on summer evenings and—most important—the cachet of an address near or "on" the park.

Although she may not have admired the park's beauty, Sigrid knew there were others who did; who were, in fact, willing to pay exorbitant rents or taxes for houses with a view—even a diagonal one—of Central Park. A shocking waste of money in her opinion, but Riley Quinn's bank balance must have been comfortable enough. The City University of New York paid its full professors generously, and as a leading expert on modern art, he'd probably done quite well financially with books, articles and outside lecture fees. Moreover, Leyden's and Vance's remarks suggested that Quinn had realized rather large sums from the sale of some of the Hungarian's paintings. Was there a motive in that? Murder to stop the sale of a dead artist's work?

Sigrid didn't actually expect much help from Quinn's widow. Regretfully she was forced to concede that this did not look like the usual simple uncomplicated "family" murder, so that Mrs. Quinn was not an active suspect. Still her comments might throw a different light on Quinn's character. Although everyone Sigrid had talked to so far said that Riley Quinn had been sarcastic, pompous and condescending, it was possible that in the privacy of his home he had been a confiding husband, had lain in his wife's arms and in the quiet darkness spoken of those who had reason to hate him.

Whenever Sigrid tried to picture living in close communion with someone, imagination failed her. She had read widely, of course, but she had no firsthand knowledge of how married people behaved when alone. Her father was a vivid memory: laughter; being swung up on his shoulders; the smell of his freshly shaven face; standing at the window to wave goodbye to him in his blue uniform—all this she remembered. But she'd been much too young to evaluate his relationship with her mother before he was killed; and Anne had never remarried, so Sigrid had nothing tangible to build on.

Of all her married cousins, north *and* south of the Mason-Dixon line, only three or four had made it through to a fifth wedding anniversary. Yes, her career had brought plenty of opportunity to see the mechanics of marriages in all strata of society, but she realized that police work presented a lopsided—and unrealistically grim—view of life and marriage.

Whatever the status of Quinn's marriage, Sigrid wasn't to hear Mrs. Quinn's version that night. As she reached for the bell, the heavy oak door suddenly swung open, spilling light across the threshold, and Oscar Nauman's tall frame filled the doorway.

Behind him stretched a hallway paneled in gleaming walnut. An intricate Tiffany lamp stood upon a richly carved chest beneath the wainscot of a wide staircase, and muted Oriental rugs softened the marble tiles. In this traditional setting the large canvases that adorned the walls looked like so many garish comic-book illustrations to Sigrid's untrained eyes, and seemed to strike a jarring note.

"Come to question the grieving widow?" asked Nauman sardonically when he had recognized her.

"Yes. Is she in?"

Nauman leaned against the door frame to consider her question. His face was shadowed, but light gleamed through his white hair and haloed his head in silver.

"Technically she's in; metaphysically she's out," he said at last.

"The technical side will be sufficient," she said coldly and started to pass him.

She was blocked by a surprisingly strong arm, and his keen blue eyes were amused at her sudden irritation. Sigrid glared back at him, and he dropped his arm to herald her entrance with a sweeping flourish of his tall lean body.

"Up the stairs and first door to your left," he called after her. "Don't say you weren't warned."

Unreasonably annoyed, Sigrid strode up the steps, her back rigid. She was conscious of Nauman's mocking eyes following her progress. At the top of the landing a concealed spotlight illuminated a small canvas chastely framed by unadorned wooden strips. At first glance it seemed to be nothing but a matte black square; not even a brush stroke disturbed its smooth surface, and its pointlessness fueled her annoyance.

As a child, she had been dutifully marched around the city's great museums, shifting from one leg to the other as her mother lectured on the aesthetic quality of one interminable picture after another. Only the portraits had held her attention, and she particularly liked the drawings and illuminated manuscripts at the Morgan Library. Still lifes and landscapes, if not too fulsome, had also been acceptable. But whenever Anne tried to interest her in nonrepresentational art, she had resisted fiercely. Once when confronted with some paintings by Jackson Pollock, she had rebelled, declared the whole room to be filled with "scribble-scrabble baby pictures" and had so dug in her heels that Anne gave up. Even a required college survey course in art appreciation had not altered her original evaluation. She still felt that abstract art was an elaborate put-on, and this plain black square before her seemed to prove it. She dismissed it with a shrug and looked around.

The rest of the upper hall was in darkness except for a sliver of light beneath the first door. Sigrid tapped softly, and at her slight pressure the door slid open upon an injudicious blend of Parisian bordello and American "sweet sixteen."

Sigrid's first stunned impression of Doris Quinn's bedroom was of its overpowering fluffiness. Bouffant white silk shades capped each delicate crystal lamp, and at all the windows heavily ruffled curtains crisscrossed beneath red velvet drapes and swags. An overstuffed chaise

longue was upholstered in some sort of white fur heaped
with plush velvet cushions, while the dressing table was
swathed in frilly white organza. Sigrid's feet sank alarm-
ingly into the soft red carpet, and her eyes were assaulted
by coy bouquets of red-and-green roses spangled across
a white wallpaper.

The bed, an extravaganza in beknobbed and curli-
cued brass, had a curved tester and dust ruffles of lace-
edged organza. The puffed silk coverlet repeated the
wallpaper's overblown roses, and it, too, was edged in
white lace, as were the pillows.

In the midst of this froth of white lace Sigrid recognized Piers Leyden's muscular form as he struggled
with a woman's inert body.

"Ah, the hell with it!" she heard him mutter. Then
he heaved himself upright and staggered over to collapse
on the chaise longue.

"Professor Leyden?" she asked hesitantly.

He smiled up at her without really focusing, turned
over and buried his curly black head in the velvet
cushions. "All classes are canceled," he announced and
promptly passed out.

From the direction of the bed rose a muffled snore.
Sigrid tiptoed over, nearly tripping on the thick rug. It
was like walking on marshmallows.

Doris Quinn was visible only from the waist down.
A black elastic girdle smoothly encased her softly rounded
bottom, and the shapely legs, which dangled over the
edge of the bed, still wore sheer black stockings. Her
head, arms and upper torso were entangled in a lacy
black slip. Frustrated in his effort to remove it, Leyden
had abandoned in midstream the whole idea of putting
Doris Quinn to bed.

If she spent the entire night with her head and arms
so constricted by that slip, Sigrid reflected, Mrs. Quinn
was going to wake up awfully stiff and sore—that is,
assuming she didn't suffocate during the night. Deftly
she extricated the rest of Doris from the slip and was

rewarded by another snore and an overpowering aroma of liquor, mingled with expensive perfume.

With the slip removed from her head, Doris Quinn was unveiled as a well-tended forty, who probably waged a daily battle with calories, but whose slight plumpness had doubtless helped keep her soft white skin so smooth and unwrinkled. Her tousled tresses were unnaturally blond but too expertly managed to show anything so crass as dark roots. Altogether a small and cuddly, pampered, indulged and thoroughly sexual woman. The kind that always made Sigrid feel gawky even though scornful of so much feminine artifice.

Irritably she turned down the covers and rolled Doris Quinn under, tucked her in, then firmly closed the rose-bud mouth. She glanced over at Piers Leyden, comatose on the furry chaise, shrugged and switched off all but one of the ruffled lamps before tiptoeing to the door. A final and distinctly unfeminine snore goaded her into banging the door shut behind her.   .

On the landing she paused again to glare at that offensive black painting. What on earth had impelled Quinn (and after seeing his wife's taste in bedroom furnishings, she was sure it *was* Quinn) to give wall space to something so meaningless? And not just wall space. He must have paid an electrician quite a bit to custom wire that concealed spotlight high in the ceiling.

But even as she frowned at the picture, she became aware of hidden depths beneath its smooth surface. The longer she stared, the more there was to see. Instead of being one shade of matte black, the painting was actually a harmonious blend of transparent blacks and browns; and each subtle tonal difference assumed a different geometric form, the shapes seeming to float in a dark void, shifting and realigning to form a rich angular pattern.

She looked away, and the canvas resumed its blank surface. She concentrated, and again veiled complexities revealed themselves. Sigrid was obscurely pleased by its

elusive beauty and came downstairs in a much better
humor than when she'd gone up.

Her crossness returned, though, when she stepped
out into the cool spring evening and found Oscar Nauman
lounging against her car, a cold pipe clenched between
his teeth.

"I thought you'd gone."

"How the hell could I go?" His crossness matched
hers. "One of your damned cohorts towed my car away
again."

"And there are no taxis?" she inquired sweetly.

"Be my guest," he offered, sourly gesturing toward
the busy avenue.

Feeling vastly superior, Sigrid walked the few steps
to the corner, stepped to the curb edge beneath a streetlight and signaled an oncoming cab. It ignored her. As
did the next two. The following four were either occupied
or displayed off-duty signs.

Annoyed, she took out the brass whistle she carried
in her shoulder bag and blew several sharp blasts. The
only response this elicited was from an excited little Scot-
tish terrier out for an evening stroll along the avenue,
which jerked the leash free from its master's hand and
bounded down the sidewalk to dance around Sigrid's feet
and jump up at her knees.

"Oh, dear! Oh, I'm *so* sorry!" apologized the owner,
a plump little man in a tweed jacket with leather patches
at the elbows, who bustled up to collect the bouncing
animal. "Heel, Mischief! Heel, I say! It's the whistle,
you see," he told Sigrid in a clipped English accent.
"She blows it—sit, Miss! My daughter, I mean. It's her
signal—sit, you naughty dog—when it's time for a romp.
For the dog I mean. Come along, Mischief. No, that's
not Sally. That's a strange lady."

The man moved away, still admonishing his dog;
and Nauman, his sense of humor restored, broke into
rich deep laughter. "That's a strange lady, that is," he
repeated in a burlesqued cockney accent.

Wryly Sigrid pocketed the whistle. She walked back

down to her car, unlocked it and said, "Get in, and I'll give you a lift downtown. I need to talk to you anyhow."

"Only on condition that we stop for dinner first. I haven't had mine yet, and you probably wouldn't be so bitchy if you'd had yours." He climbed in beside her, and she was aware of a clean smell of turpentine and mellow tobacco. A not unpleasant combination.

"I'm not a health-food, wheat-germ addict," she warned nastily, turning the ignition key.

"Neither am I," he answered serenely. "I had in mind a thick and bloody steak."

7

As twilight fell the spring evening was infused with a pervasive moistness somewhat between a heavy dew and a thin fog. It haloed streetlights and gave the air a soft texture that would make country-reared, transplanted city dwellers remember seedtime and spring rains. Restless with vague yearnings for new-turned earth, they would drift home from work tomorrow instead of rushing along in their usual blind fashion. Their eyes would see what they had previously ignored: flats of petunias, marigolds, candytuft and salvia displayed for sale in front of a dozen different stores. And many a New Yorker, suddenly and unaccountably homesick for the green fields of Kentucky, Ohio, or Minnesota, would stop and buy as many tender seedlings as his bit of earth— be it only a single narrow window box—could accommodate. "You can take the boy out of the country . . ." they would tell each other sheepishly as they exchanged advice on potting soils and tomato varieties.

There was no gateway into Central Park opposite the street Quinn's brownstone stood on, only tall iron railings. Behind the railings, in the deepest shadows where the illumination of one mist-blurred streetlight barely met the next, stood a man. He was concealed from casual notice by the thickly overgrown bushes, which pushed tender twigs through the rails in front of him. From his camouflaged position he had a clear view across the wide avenue and down the side street to the third house from the corner—Quinn's house—from which a trickle of people had been coming and going since he arrived late that afternoon.

He had watched Sigrid Harald's attempt to whistle down a cab for Professor Nauman; and when they had finally driven away, he was fairly certain no one remained in the house except Riley Quinn's widow. Nevertheless, he patiently waited another half hour to be sure, then made his way through the dew-wet bushes to the nearest park exit half a block away and from there to Quinn's front door. At last, abandoning all signs of his previous stealth, he marched boldly up the broad stone steps.

Distracted by finding Nauman still there when she emerged earlier, Sigrid had not noticed that the latch was off, so the knob turned smoothly under the intruder's gloved hand, and he didn't need the crowbar he carried concealed in his jacket sleeve.

He slipped inside and closed the door even more quietly than he'd opened it. No one challenged his entry. No sound reached him at all, in fact, apart from the muted traffic noises from outside. He felt he could handle Mrs. Quinn, but it was simpler if the point didn't arise.

Lamps had been left lighted throughout the house. The intruder glanced disdainfully at the paintings that had looked like cartoons to Sigrid, scrutinized their signatures, then passed down the entry hall into a spacious living room stale with the odors of cigarette butts and a spilled bottle of Scotch. Someone had made a stab at tidying up, had gathered dirty ashtrays and emptied cocktail glasses onto a large wood tray that had been left on an open liquor cabinet. There were still ice cubes in the silver ice bucket and open bottles of every persuasion stood about.

Everywhere he turned, there were more drawings and paintings. He circled the room like a nearsighted museum visitor, then toured the dining room, the butler's pantry and, briefly, the kitchen. No sign of what he'd come for. He moved back into the living room and considered the stairs. Perhaps up there? But Mrs. Quinn was up there, too.

He hesitated, undecided, then noticed an inconspicuous door, paneled like the rest of the entry hall, just beneath the stairs. He opened it, groped in darkness, and lights came on inside Riley Quinn's study.

The room was windowless, about fourteen feet square and had probably started life as a storage area. Whatever its origin, it now looked like something ordered from an office-furniture catalog: "one middle-class study, college-professor type." A leather-topped desk stood before the rear wall. Nearby were a leather swivel desk chair and matching leather armchairs, a globe stand, a large dictionary on its own little table and several brass lamps. The door wall held framed diplomas and various certificates of honor interspersed with small engravings. The two side walls were lined with glass-fronted mahogany bookcases filled with books.

For all his posing, Quinn had been a diligent worker. On his desk were an electric typewriter and several folders with the nearly completed manuscript of his latest book. Behind the desk, on the fourth wall, was a section devoted to slide-sized wooden files, each drawer labeled by dates, artists or movements. Beside them was a built-in viewing counter of frosted glass, which could be lit from beneath whenever Quinn wanted to arrange the slide sequence of a lecture.

A bank of letter-size file cabinets three drawers tall formed a continuation of the counter. Again they were of the same dark wood, and on the front of each drawer was a brass-rimmed card holder with detailed labels of content. It was to these that the intruder was drawn after his careful examination of the bookcases yielded nothing tangible.

He found the section of the alphabet that interested him, set his crowbar in a corner and tugged at a drawer pull. It opened with a harsh squeak, and the man froze, listening for alarms.

From upstairs came only a muffled duet of snores.

Sandy Keppler's apartment building was near Tompkins Square, and had been built around the turn of the century in a more expansive age when every household comprised several children and at least one live-in servant girl. Back then a single floor barely sufficed for a proper apartment. Now each room was a separate efficiency and considered spacious by modern standards.

Much of the original molding and all of the oak flooring, admittedly a bit scarred by now, remained. Sandy kept hers waxed to a glossy sheen and bare except for a few inexpensive scatter rugs. She had painted all the walls herself and had even installed the folding shutters that closed off a tiny kitchenette. Bright cushions were heaped on a blue couch that opened into a double bed, and since this had once been a front parlor, the room boasted a charming bay window whose curve was just big enough to hold a small table, two chairs and several hanging baskets of begonias, all in full bloom.

It was a cheerful, homey room, her toehold on New York, and Sandy hated the idea of leaving it. Idaho, for God's sake! It would be worse than that upstate small town she'd escaped from two years ago.

Although she would insist it didn't affect her, Sandy came from a long line of nest builders. One may shake from one's feet the dust of a small town one considers provincial and stultifying; shaking off heredity is another thing altogether. Sandy's father had worried about all the dangers—physical and moral—faced by a young girl alone in the big city; but her mother had come down, taken a good look at the apartment and relaxed, knowing her daughter's values were unchanged.

A totally liberated woman, thought Mrs. Keppler, does not collect casserole recipes, buy furniture with an eye toward how it'll fit into a larger apartment "someday" nor after only a year on her own begin every other sentence with "David says . . ."

Mrs. Keppler was quite confident that she'd dance at her daughter's wedding yet.

As she cleared the last dishes from the table and blew out the candles, Sandy glanced over at David, who was correcting a batch of themes from one of Professor

Simpson's classes. He lounged on her blue couch, his
glasses riding precariously down on the end of his nose,
one foot propped on an old brass and wood trunk she'd
bought at a thrift shop, and which served as both coffee
table and linen closet.

He looked very domestic, and while washing up
their few dishes, Sandy briefly considered mentioning
that tonight's spaghetti dinner had cost less than fifty
cents a serving. Not that it would change his mind. No
more than would the argument that he should go ahead
and move in with her since he spent more time here
than in his own apartment and could be saving that two
hundred and fifty in rent. Maintaining certain appear-
ances was part of David's old-fashioned code of morality,
though he was modern enough in other ways, she reminded herself with a satisfied grin.

The object of her thoughts suddenly exploded in
outraged sensibilities.

"Listen to this!" he commanded, pushing his glasses
back up where they belonged. " 'The ancient Romans
were really hip to all kinds of modern jazz. Like their
houses had central heat, hot and cold running water, and
you could flush the johns, and since they dug being clean
so much, they had great big public bathrooms where
everybody grooved together a couple of times a day.' "

"Well, didn't they?" Sandy teased. She put the last
plate in the drainer, dried her hands and came in to join
him on the blue couch.

"Technically, yes. At least the wealthiest classes had
all that; but this jive-talking illiterate makes it sound as
if everyone had oil furnaces in the basement and electric
water heaters on every floor. And the Romans didn't
bathe every day just because they 'dug being clean so
much'!"

He scrawled a bitter comment across the top of the
unfortunate theme and added a grade: *C* ·for facts; *F*-
minus for composition. "And how the hell he ever passed
English 1.1 is beyond me," he muttered. From the lofty

height of his twenty-four years came fretful predictions for the imminent demise of education.

Sandy knelt beside him and gently smoothed his hair as he picked up another paper and began to read.

"Sensuous old Romans," she murmured. "All that bathing just for the fun of it."

Her fingers moved down to the nape of his neck and hesitated provocatively. David Wade's breathing quickened, but he kept his eyes firmly fixed on the papers before him.

She leaned away then and casually twisted her long golden hair into an enchanting topknot. "As long as you're working, I think I'll go take a shower myself."

Her tone was innocent, but her dimples beguiled as she loosened the top button of her blouse. David abandoned his papers and pulled her down to him. She laughed, pretended to pull away; yet all her struggles only seemed to twist her into more kissable positions. Somehow in the next few minutes his glasses became entangled in her hair, but neither noticed.

"Want me to soap your back?" he murmured, nibbling a dainty pink ear.

"What about those themes? What'll you tell Professor Simpson tomorrow?"

"The truth," he grinned, feeling a joyous virility rising within. " 'The woman tempted me, and the fruit I did eat thereof'—or however that quotation goes!"

As the subway roared away from Franklin Avenue, Harley Harris roused himself enough to wonder which Seventh Avenue express he was on. The evening rush hour was long past, and he nearly had the car to himself, but he'd been riding and changing trains so aimlessly these last few hours that he'd lost track. Flatbush or New Lots, which was it? The interior sign by the door was broken. Jammed permanently at Pelham Bay. No help there.

The door at the end of the car opened, and an emaciated drunk weaved through. Swaying with the motion of the train, he steadied himself on the pole beside Harley, and a fetid smell of cheap wine and urine settled around them. The drunk wore a dingy overcoat three sizes too large, baggy green pants and brand-new black-and-white sneakers. His gray crew cut was a month late for the barber's chair, and he did not appear to have a shirt or teeth.

"Gimme a dollar," he told Harley.

The boy slid down to the end of the empty bench. The drunk followed, stumbling from one overhead strap to another till he dangled in front of Harley again. "Gimme a dollar," he repeated.

Harley Harris stared straight ahead, ignoring him.

"How 'bout a quarter, then?" asked the drunk.

"Leave me alone!" Harley said shrilly.

The drunk lost his handhold and half lurched, half fell the length of the car, fetching up by a pair of well-dressed matrons who appeared to be coming home from an afternoon of shopping followed by dinner out. One carried a dress box from Lane Bryant, the other a smaller Saks box. Both regarded the unshaven, ill-smelling derelict with distinct disapproval.

"Gimme a dollar," Harley heard him say.

"Go to hell," advised the first matron.

The second followed with an explicit but anatomically impossible suggestion. Shocked, the drunk retreated to a corner seat, muttering to himself.

Harley looked at his watch. Almost ten. He'd had nothing to eat since a hot dog and bagel at Grand Central his third or fourth time through. When had that been? Two o'clock? Three? And there was his old man expecting him at three to help lay out the summer display windows for the Susie-Lynne stores. He'd probably be standing on his head by now.

Every time he thought about what he'd done, Harley Harris felt queasy. Nauman had it coming to him, he told himself; but the anger that had fueled him earlier had dissipated, and now he was wondering if maybe he'd acted too hastily. Too drastically. If only he'd waited and *made* Nauman talk to him, artist to artist.

That's what his old man was always saying: "Harley, you don't think what you're doing till you've done it."

The train slowed down, stopped, and the two matrons got off.

"They weren't no ladies," the drunk confided to the car at large, but Harley Harris was twisting to look for signs.

Kingston. Good, he was on the New Lots train after all. Home was only five minutes away, and dinner would have been saved for him. Suddenly he felt like a small boy again. Mom would cry and smear her glasses; the old man would storm and rage, but Harley was too tired to care anymore.

I'll tell Pop, he thought. Pop'll figure out what I should do.

All his life Pop had told him what to do. Post-graduate work had been his first rebellion; and now his heart sank even lower, knowing what his stern father would probably make him do.

8

Madigan's was another relic of New York's bygone days, a sort of unofficial memorial to a lustier, roughneck age. Located in a seamy section near the docks south of Fourteenth Street, the tavern had outlasted wars, depressions, recessions, Prohibition and several attempts at urban renewal. Its original customers had been sailors, draymen and Irish stevedores working on the piers; and for the first eighty years of its existence only one female had ever been served there: Madame Ernestine Schumann-Heink.

The famous opera star had just disembarked from the ship that had returned her to America for another season at the Metropolitan when the horse drawing her carriage went lame practically on Madigan's threshold. It was late fall with a chill rain falling. His chivalry appealed to, Francis Madigan (son of "Daddy" Madigan, the founder) had reluctantly offered his tavern as a waiting room for her party while another horse was being fetched.

There were dark looks upon her entrance; two or three old-timers standing at the long mahogany bar had muttered into their ale about "petticoat patronage" and with ostentatious rudeness had given her their backs. But the great contralto was then at the height of her powers and had accurately sized up her "house"—child's play to a woman who would still be able to sing in *Das Rheingold* when she was sixty-four.

She began with the few Celtic lullabies at her disposal and, when those were exhausted, switched to the sweetest German songs in her repertoire. The language barrier evaporated—sentimentality has never needed translation—and soon the most hard-bitten stevedores were weeping into their glasses. (Empty glasses, one might add, since no one had wanted to break the spell to order.) For over an hour the majestic Schumann-Heink held them in the palm of her queenly hand until at last she expressed fatigue and impatience at the nonarrival of a fresh horse; whereupon a dozen strong men hitched themselves to her carriage and pulled it though the rain all the way to her hotel on Seventh Avenue.

"Shure and she was a foine lady," said the pragmatic Francis Madigan, tallying up the evening's lost revenues, "but women do be taking a man's mind off his drinking."

Succeeding owners, even those not of Irish descent, had echoed his sentiments, and Madigan's was one of the last male bastions to fall beneath the feminist assault. Not that women came there very often once their point was made. Madigan's was not quaint, picturesque, or cozy. In point of fact, it was quite hopelessly shabby, for there had been few concessions to modernity. Women were, by law, tolerated; but they were not encouraged with any plastic niceties.

No wine, beer, or liquor was served. Dark stout and porter foamed down the sides of chunky glass mugs, and food arrived on chipped brown earthenware, while the wide oak tables and benches were so dingy with age and indifferent cleaning that the sawdust on the floor looked fresh by comparison. The air was thick with stale malt fumes and greasy smoke, and Sigrid Harald peered through it dubiously.

"I can see at least a dozen violations of the health code from right here. God knows what the kitchen must look like."

"A policewoman shouldn't quibble about minor dangers," said Nauman. "I thought you wanted the best steak in town."

"Not if it comes with a side order of ptomaine," she said tartly.

Their waiter had a poor grasp of English, but he flashed a gold-toothed smile, eager to please. "You no worry about that, *señora*. We no have it—just plain lettuce for the *ensalada*."

Sigrid laughed, and a certain familiar curve of her lips pricked the artist's memory.

"Harald," he said reflectively when the waiter had taken their order and gone. "Are you by any chance related to a photojournalist, Anne Harald?"

"My mother," Sigrid said, and her lips tightened defensively as she waited for the inevitable, disparaging comparison. Anne Harald was known for her vivacious beauty, and casual acquaintances found it difficult to think of this tall, plain young woman as her daughter.

Instead Nauman said only, "She took some pictures of my work for a *Life* article years ago. Good camera work."

"Were you in that series?" Sigrid asked, surprised. Then she realized her gaucherie. "I'm sorry. Of course, you would have been. That was the whole point of the piece, wasn't it? Profiles of leading American artists. I was away at school when my mother was working on it, so I'm afraid I don't remember any of the details."

"You might want to look it up since Riley Quinn wrote the accompanying text. Your mother writes most of her own stuff now, doesn't she? Haven't seen her in years, but wasn't she nominated for a Pulitzer not too long ago?"

Sigrid nodded. "For a story on how Vietnamese refugees are assimilating into this culture. She keeps an apartment here, but she doesn't use it much. She's all over the world these days, taking pictures about issues with more social significance."

"Meaning that art has none?" Nauman asked, amused.

"Well, does it?"

"Very little," he admitted wryly. "But not for any reasons you might give."

"Probably not. Of course, I don't know very much about art, but—"

"Oh, Lord! You're not going to say it?" he groaned.

"—but I know what I like," she finished firmly.

"She said it!" Nauman mourned to the waiter, who'd just arrived with their steaks.

The waiter beamed uncomprehendingly and deftly distributed their dinner dishes. As promised, the salad had no romaine lettuce, just wilted iceberg under an indifferent bottled dressing; but the baked potatoes had crisp jackets and had been split open to receive huge dollops of butter, while the man-sized steaks still sizzled, and small streams of deep red juices trickled from several fork pricks.

Sigrid suddenly remembered that she hadn't eaten since early morning, and when Nauman insisted that she try an anchovy, she was too hungry to resist. With that first taste of a steak grilled to absolute perfection she instantly forgave the greasy table and smoky air, the food-specked menus and crazed earthenware dishes. And the salty anchovies were such a delicious complement to red meat that she might even have forgiven Nauman's condescension had he not tactlessly brought it up again.

"Very well, Lietenant, what kind of art do you like?"

"Pictures of people."

"Norman Rockwell?" he jeered.

"No." She speared another anchovy.

Nauman studied her intently, feeling slightly annoyed. Taken separately, the features of the young woman across the table were excellent: strong facial bones, clear skin, extraordinary gray eyes, dark hair that tried to escape from its braided knot, and a wide mouth shaped for generous laughter. Yet collectively her features might as well have added up to total gracelessness for all the use she put them to.

Despite his fame Oscar Nauman was not an arrogant man; still without realizing it, he had become spoiled. He was used to having women make an effort to amuse him. As his reputation had grown in the past thirty years, so had the number of women who sought him out. He was cynical enough to know why many came—the would-be artists, the bored faculty wives, the semi-intellectual sophisticates, all drawn like moths to the flame of his public recognition—but he had attracted women before he became well known, and an innocent pride in his own masculinity made him think he knew why the ones he chose had stayed.

Nor had his relations with every female been purely physical. Among his closest friends were many women whose minds he respected, who could hold their own in fierce intellectual debate. But even with these, there had been an initial period in which they had probed and tested each other, an exchanged awareness of sexuality. Sublimated, yes, but quite definitely there.

With Sigrid Harald he felt none of these subtle nuances, and it piqued him. She seemed as sexless as a young boy. For a brief moment he wondered if he were getting too old; then his subconscious pride discarded that hypothesis and flicked onto other reasons. Could she be frigid? A lesbian? Or had she been too early or too bitterly rejected? Was her prickly facade merely a thick shell covering a romantic nature? He rather favored that last theory and thought it might be interesting to prove.

"Renaissance portraits, right?" (In his experience most closet romantics loved the Renaissance.) "Botticelli, Raphael, Michelangelo?"

"Some of them," she admitted. "But my favorites— do you know those pen-and-ink heads by Dürer? And Holbein? And especially those drawings by Lucas Cranach?"

"The Goths?" Nauman was astounded. His memory conjured up those north-European masters of the late Middle Ages. The sober and pure linear quality of their work. He had thought to furnish this odd young woman's mind with romanticism, gorgeous costumes and rich colors; but she had outreached him, stripped away all non-essentials and retreated to the uncluttered simplicity and elegance of late Gothic line and form.

"I told you I don't know much about art," Sigrid said tightly as he broke into delighted laughter.

"I'm not laughing at you but at myself. For jumping to unwarranted conclusions." If she could respond to the austere directness of these drawings . . . There seemed to be more to this unusual policewoman than he'd suspected.

He put on his most charming air and tried to draw her out, but his laughter had offended. She ate neatly but swiftly with the air of one who'd had to leave more than one meal unfinished.

Nettled, Nauman concentrated on his own steak. "I might have known you wouldn't like anything created in this century," he said crossly.

"Actually you're wrong." The steak had been surprisingly good, the ale refreshing, and now that Nauman had quit trying to be charming, Sigrid felt more at ease. "I saw a small black and brown painting at the Quinn house just tonight. On the top landing. Do you know it?"

"Are you putting me on?" he asked suspiciously.

"Why? Isn't it any good, either?" Enlightenment dawned in her gray eyes. "Oh. Is it yours?"

He nodded. "I did that thirty years ago, but it was damn good. You've just made it impossible for me to attack your taste."

"Excellent. Perhaps now we can quit pretending this is a social occasion and get down to work."

She pushed aside the dishes and opened her ubiquitous notebook. "You must have known Professor Quinn as well as anyone. Who'd want him dead? Leyden?"

"Because of that tableau you saw with Doris Quinn?"

"They did seem . . . intimate."

Nauman smiled at the chasteness of the term. "If Piers Leyden wanted Riley Quinn dead, it wouldn't be because of Doris. She was just extra protection."

"Against what?"

"Against what Quinn was likely to say about Leyden in his latest book." Nauman toyed with his mug, creating patterns of wet, interlocking circles on the wooden tabletop as he chose his words carefully.

"Riley was a bastard," he said slowly, "but he knew a hell of a lot about art trends since the war, and he didn't hesitate to make value judgments. If he said your work had merit, you'd stop having trouble getting a gallery to show it. If he said it was good, you'd start selling occasionally. And if he called it of lasting value, you'd sell things regularly, and people would come around to your studio begging you to accept their commissions.

"There's been so much crap floating around these past few years—pop, op, slop—that collectors with more money than confidence in their own taste depend on someone like Riley. It's similar to what Bernard Berenson did for Renaissance art. It's all very well to buy a trendy piece of art because it amuses you; but if a Riley Quinn approves, then it becomes a good investment, too."

"Like having someone tell you Picasso's going to be Picasso before he actually becomes Picasso, and the prices go up," Sigrid said thoughtfully. "And Quinn didn't consider Professor Leyden a Picasso?"

"You do have a talent for understatement," Nauman smiled. "Leyden's a good draftsman, and he knows more about anatomy and the way muscles work than most doctors, but he doesn't have much taste.

"Ordinarily that wouldn't matter," he added cynically. "His things are probably better than many of Riley's pets, but Quinn and Leyden have always clashed—one of those natural antipathies—and Quinn was planning to put him down for all time in his new book. I suppose Leyden thought that bedding Doris would take the edge off Quinn's attack, make everyone think Riley Quinn was letting personalities influence his judgment. Which he was, of course, but not because of Doris."

"How will Quinn's death affect the book?"

Nauman's eyes narrowed, and his speech became telegraphic as his mind zipped through possibilities. "Final draft . . . on the other hand . . . intestate . . . and Saxer's hungry enough, God knows."

He sipped his ale moodily, and Sigrid struggled to catch up with him. Final draft—well, that was clear enough: the book was finished but not yet at the publishers. If Quinn hadn't left a will, that would make Doris Quinn his literary executor, too.

"So if there are things Piers Leyden wants changed, Mrs. Quinn can force Jake Saxer to rewrite those parts now?"

"That's what I said!" Nauman snapped.

Sigrid's eyebrows lifted. She saw this reaction frequently when decent people involved in an investigation suddenly realized that a person they knew had committed murder, and that they were being asked to help hunt that person down—to trap him, knowing that the guilty one might be a friend or colleague. With that initial awareness came anger, a reluctance to betray anyone and a shrinking away in distaste.

His reaction made Nauman seem human and vulnerable; and for the first time since meeting him, Sigrid was conscious of the man's age. He had such a forceful personality that she hadn't noticed it before. His white hair was not just the famous Nauman trademark; the lines in his face did not denote character only. They were milestones from days and months of living that added up to years. With an unexpected feeling of regret she realized that he was old—that his first recognized masterpiece must have been painted years before she'd even been born.

There were brown age marks on the backs of his hands. But even as she saw them she noted the vigorous body, saw that the fingers that steadied his pipe were sensate and strong; and when he laid his pipe aside and impatiently raked his thick white hair with those fingers, it seemed absurd to think of him as anything but ageless, no matter what the calendars said.

"So you think one of us poisoned Riley Quinn?" he asked, referring to the group detained earlier that day. "One of those six?"

"Eight if you count Harley Harris and Mike Szabo. I'm still not sure how Quinn's death would benefit Szabo, but from what Professor Ross and Miss Keppler say, he did have opportunity."

"Mike has a hot temper," Nauman objected. "Poisoning would be too deliberate for him."

Sigrid reserved judgment and asked, "If Janos Karoly was an important artist, why is his nephew working as a janitor?"

"Important artists come from all classes of society, Lieutenant, and they seldom make much money till after they're dead," Nauman said bitterly. "Then it's the entrepreneurs and promoters like Riley who cash in on their works. Do you know Karoly's paintings?"

Sigrid shook her head. "No. I think I've heard the name, but you were right when you guessed that twentieth-century art doesn't much interest me."

Perversely he was pleased that she didn't apologize or make a pretense of excepting his work. He had always preferred indifference over the empty flattery of someone who hadn't the least understanding of what he was striving for. Open hostility would be even better because anger implied that the viewer took the work seriously enough to feel challenged by Nauman's assumptions.

Their waiter returned to clear the table, and by this time Sigrid was so used to the tavern's scruffy ambience that it didn't outrage her to see him use one corner of his dirty apron to wipe it dry before setting down the tray of coffee utensils.

Nauman stirred sugar into his cup, drew on his pipe and leaned back in the heavy oak chair. He hoped he wasn't getting pedantic. That was the danger when one was so innately a teacher; it was so hard not to lecture. Especially when one's audience was as receptive as this policewoman seemed to be.

"Janos Karoly," he said slowly, "was probably Riley Quinn's one foray into altruism. It turned out so profitably that it's always puzzled me that he never tried it again. Unless Mike Szabo's right, and it wasn't honest altruism.

"It all started after the war." He paused and looked at Sigrid's face. Only around her eyes and at the corners of her mouth were there faint beginnings of age lines.

"The Second World War," he clarified carefully. "There had been a few abstract exhibitions before the war, but abstract expressionism didn't arrive until '46 and '47. Paris was still the international art center of the world, and everyone went there. The great, the near great and the merely hopeful—Soulages, Hartung, Poliakoff, Appel—and not just artists but critics and historians. Riley, too, clutching his discharge papers from the *Stars and Stripes* and looking for firsthand data for his post-graduate studies."

"*Stars and Stripes* was a military newspaper, wasn't it?"

"Right. He'd been one of the feature writers on the staff. That was before I met him, but we were all the same—lusty young cockerels playing King of the Mountain on the art heaps of Paris. Janos Karoly was there, and one of the more established artists. A fairly respected practitioner of tachism, though not really in the master ranks."

"What's tachism?" she asked.

"Literally it means spot painting. Refers to the way an artist puts paint on a canvas. Someone more calligraphic might brush on wide slashes and bands of color. A tachist adds spot to spot or wedge to wedge and—"

"I thought that was called impressionism," Sigrid objected. "Like what's his name? Seurat?"

"Seurat used very small pellets of color, and his pictures were all quite representational. Something like newspaper pictures built up of black dots. The tachists were abstract, and in the purest examples their pictures became loosely structured clusters and patches of color. They downplayed line to concentrate on color and texture.

"That's the way Karoly was painting when Riley first met him. It was all very competent, but nothing to set your blood on fire. Still he was almost sixty then, and he'd knocked around Europe long enough to have known everyone—Braque, Picasso, Matisse, Kandinsky, all the Bauhaus people—and Riley was impressed. What Karoly thought of Riley . . . well, he had an acid tongue, but Riley's French was limited, and his Hungarian nonexistent, so Karoly's choicest remarks went over his head. Things were never as bad in Paris as they were in other European capitals, but there were still shortages and rationing, and the black market was expensive. With his American dollars and his American military connections Riley could wangle extra amenities. Karoly allowed him to bring food and wine and coal and sit in his studio and listen to him reminisce about art and artists. I suppose it was mutually beneficial.

"At last, though, Riley came back to finish his dissertation, and Karoly decided he was an old man who should die in his native land, although I believe Hungary was the one European country he'd assiduously avoided for the previous forty-five years. Nobody heard from him after that. If they thought of him at all, it was probably to assume that he was dead. Then came the Hungarian Revolution. Were you old enough to remember that?"

"I remember," Sigrid said, ignoring his allusion to age. "Tanks and people running in the streets."

"How Janos Karoly got mixed up in the political mess, no one could ever understand. He didn't even know himself—maybe they thought his paintings were too decadent, who can say? His name wound up on a proscribed list, but somehow he got out of the country and into Italy, and the first person he ran into was Riley Quinn, who was in Rome appraising some things for the Klaustadt Gallery when Karoly wandered in with a roll of canvases under his arm. Riley took one look and immediately talked him into applying for an American visa. He arranged the flight and found him a studio."

"He could still paint? He must have been nearly seventy by then," said Sigrid, who'd been keeping track of the dates.

Nauman nodded. "I remember how he seemed older than God when I saw him then." There was wry self-mockery in his smile. "Somehow seventy doesn't sound as old as it used to."

A burst of heavy male laughter arose from a far table. The bar at the front of the deep room was well lined now with serious drinkers—longshoremen, mechanics and three crewmen from a German liner that had docked that morning. The tavern had grown warm enough to make Sigrid take off her shapeless gray jacket. Underneath was a chastely tailored white silk shirt. Man-styled with buttons down the front, pointed collar tips and close-fitting cuffs at the thin wrists, it had survived a day of city grime and polluted air to remain pristinely white. As she leaned forward to pull the jacket sleeves free, the white material stretched tautly over small, high breasts, briefly outlining the lace tracery of her bra beneath.

And wasn't that interesting, thought Nauman fleetingly. All tailored and buttoned up on the outside, lace lingerie beneath. It was enough to make him revive his theory of repressed romanticism.

"If Karoly's work was only conventionally good, why would Professor Quinn go to so much trouble?" Sigrid asked. "He must have met lots of well-known artists by that time."

"You're catching on to Riley's character," Nauman approved. "You're right; he'd learned a lot since postwar Paris, and he no longer sat at any artist's feet. But Karoly was exceptional. Everyone thought he'd done all he was capable of. Very few artists go on breaking new ground in their old age, but Karoly was a maverick. When he got back to Hungary, he was very isolated from the artistic community, and somehow in his solitude he discovered a whole new wellspring of creativity within himself and completely transcended tachism. Oh, he still used the basic techniques, but he'd tightened his structure. The subjects were mostly still lifes—fruits and flowers and luminous bowls and vases. Incredible handling of color and shape. The National Gallery has six of those paintings, and they almost justify a trip to Washington. Riley did his damnedest to discourage him, but Karoly insisted on giving them to the government in gratitude for his sanctuary. Also by way of thumbing his nose at the Communist regime in Hungary." There was jaundiced cynicism in Nauman's tone.

"So far as I know—and I only saw him once or twice that last year—he never questioned why Riley would go to so much trouble and expense for him. He didn't read English, so he had no idea how strong a reputation Riley was building as an astute critic and authority. Karoly was just as arrogant and scornful as he'd been in Paris. Thought Riley was a toad but a useful toad; that he was still a star-struck admirer whose only function was to furnish food, shelter and painting materials so the master could get on with his work. It was the old biter-bit thing, but justified somehow because he was still discovering new frontiers when he died. If the Whitney weren't closed, I'd haul you over right now to see the painting that was on his easel when he died—*New World Nexus*, where unexpected representational elements begin to show up."

Nauman's coffee had grown cold, but he drank it anyhow, lost in a memory Sigrid didn't disturb. At last he sighed and picked up the thread again.

"Karoly had been here about four years when he suddenly dropped dead of a heart attack, and Riley produced a holographic will. In French, of course, but properly notarized and witnessed. Reduced to its simplest elements, it said he was leaving everything to Riley Quinn to do with as Quinn saw fit. There was one curious phrase: he wrote that he knew Quinn would do all that was '*juste et humain*' with his paintings. There were no relatives here to contest the will, so it was probated without a hitch.

"Since then Janos Karoly's reputation has got bigger every year. Riley had a genius for fanning the flames just enough. He donated three paintings to the Museum of Modern Art on condition that at least one be displayed at all times, or the gift would be revoked. That was to keep them in the public eye. Then he'd lend three or four to an exhibition here or see that they were mentioned in an important article there. He was chary about selling them, but whenever he let one go, it always brought the full asking price.

"The one thing he didn't do was let anyone touch Karoly's notebooks. Shortly after Karoly's death he'd started translating them for publication—he read French very fluently—but he complained to me once that every time Karoly seemed to be getting to the heart of a problem, he'd switch to Hungarian. Naturally I suggested getting someone to translate those passages, but he mumbled some excuse, and that was the last time he ever mentioned the notebooks willingly. He'd always change the subject if they came up."

"Where does Mike Szabo come in?" Sigrid asked as he paused to refill his coffee cup and hers from the thick earthenware pot on their table.

"That started about a year and a half ago. The Klaustadt Gallery owned a couple of Karoly's paintings, which they'd bought from Riley, and they wanted to do a retrospective. Riley made the mistake of agreeing. The show was stunning. No other word for it. It was the first time that many of Karoly's later paintings had been seen together, and they captivated the public's fancy. Inevitable, I suppose. The colors were so entrancing, and they were representational enough to be understood by most people, including the sector that usually professes itself indifferent to art."

Sigrid ignored the barb.

"The exhibition attracted wide coverage—from all the art journals and even from newsmagazines and television. Somebody started calling Karoly the 'Hungarian Picasso,' which showed an abysmal ignorance of both artists; but it stuck. About a week after that, Mike Szabo turned up at the Klaustadt and demanded to know who had stolen his uncle's paintings. Created quite a scene." Nauman grinned, recalling accounts of that laborer's eruption into Klaustadt's elegant premises, how in three or four broken languages he had called them all thieves and swindlers loudly, indignantly and at great length.

"They bundled him into a back room and sent for Riley in a hurry. Riley accused him of being an impostor at first, but he had papers and letters that proved he was definitely the only son of Janos Karoly's only sister. She'd been much younger than Karoly, and they hadn't seen each other in years; but when he fled Hungary, he'd smuggled a letter back to her, which promised that he wouldn't forget her or her son. Szabo found it among her papers after her death in '67 and immediately scurried off to Italy, but he couldn't find anyone who'd ever heard of Janos Karoly. I gather he wasn't particularly disappointed. Art in the abstract doesn't seem to appeal to him too much. He'd drifted around Europe for a while and finally wound up in Pittsburgh in the early seventies, living on the fringes of the Hungarian community there, working odd jobs and making just enough to get by. Nobody in that crowd gave a damn about art, either; but once the news media started giving so much space to their 'Hungarian Picasso,' someone mentioned it in Szabo's presence, and it sank in.

"Legally he didn't have a leg to stand on, but Quinn tried to stop it quickly and gave him five thousand dollars outright."

"Plus a one-way ticket back to Pittsburgh?" Sigrid asked dryly.

Nauman shook his head. "Riley was more thorough than that. The ticket was for Budapest with the promise of another five thousand when he arrived."

"I'm surprised Szabo didn't take it. Ten thousand must have seemed like a lot of money to an odd-jobber."

"Oh, he was tempted," Nauman conceded, "but Piers Leyden deflected him and helped him resist. Leyden was at the Klaustadt the next day, heard the whole story and saw an irresistible chance to tweak Riley's nose. He told Szabo that Riley wouldn't have given him a dime if he didn't have a guilty conscience, and that ten thousand was a pittance compared to the true worth of his uncle's paintings. Szabo was only too willing to believe it; but what could he do?"

"Leyden was no doubt full of suggestions," Sigrid said. She had taken the neo-realist's measure.

"Dozens," Nauman agreed. "For openers he advised Szabo to take the first five thousand and cash in the plane ticket. Then he got Szabo a job raking leaves and shifting furniture with Buildings and Grounds. Szabo hired a lawyer, but Karoly's will was too explicit—'everything to Riley Quinn' in black and white."

"Couldn't the lawyer make anything out of that *'juste et humain'* phrase?"

"Too nebulous."

Sigrid set down her coffee mug and said reflectively, "Szabo must have been a constant embarrassment to Professor Quinn. If it were Leyden who'd been poisoned, I know who my chief suspect would be."

"Don't be too sure," Nauman said lightly. "Leyden's addicted to practical jokes, and Riley wasn't his only victim."

Returning to her original point, Sigrid said, "You say Szabo was too emotional to poison Quinn, but what if it were something unplanned, a spur-of-the-moment yielding to temptation when he found himself alone with Quinn's coffee?"

"When was he alone with it? There were still three other cups on that tray then—mine, Sandy's and Vance's. And potassium dichromate's not something you walk around with in your pocket, is it?"

"The grounds people must have duplicates of all the keys, and he'd certainly have access to them," Sigrid pointed out reasonably, "but I suppose he couldn't have known the coffee routine any better than Harley Harris did."

"No, it couldn't have been Harris, either," said Nauman.

Was there regret in his tone, wondered Sigrid.

"Nor Sandy."

"Why not?" she asked coldly. "Are pretty little blond secretaries automatically exempt?"

A flicker of amusement touched Nauman's lips as

he noted her acerbic tone. "No motive. She and young
Wade are getting married sometime this summer; going
off to Idaho in September. She liked Simpson better than
Riley, but I can't see her killing Riley so his job could
be a going-away present for Bert Simpson. If he even
wants it. He's turned the deputy chairmanship down
once before, you know."

Something niggled in the corner of his mind.

"What is it?" she asked alertly.

Nauman shook his head. "It's gone now."

"Something to do with Simpson or Sandy Keppler?
Or what about David Wade? Could Quinn have hurt
him in any way? Maybe written a nasty letter of rec-
ommendation?"

Again Nauman shook his head but less decisively.
"No, Riley actually wrote a very flattering letter. Or
rather, he told Sandy what to say and then signed it.
Riley did run the art history side of the department, and
theoretically David Wade was answerable to him; but in
practice they had almost nothing to do with each other.
As long as the young lecturers taught their classes com-
petently, Riley left them alone. And Simpson, not Riley,
was Wade's dissertation advisor, so there'd be no conflict
in that area."

Again something niggled just below the surface of
his consciousness, but this time Nauman ignored it and
signaled for their bill.

"It's so idiotic and pointless," he said with returning
anger. "Sandy, Vance, and Harris gain absolutely nothing with Riley dead. Saxer may get his name on the book
as coauthor; Leyden will get a better mention in the
book; Andrea Ross'll be promoted; and Bert Simpson
will probably be the new deputy chairman. Is any of that
worth killing for?"

"Earlier today a boy knifed a doctor for enough drugs
to feed his habit for two days," said Sigrid dryly. "Was
that worth killing for?"

"A doped-up hophead's different!" On his feet now,
Nauman towered over her. He slapped a bill down on

the table to cover their check. "These are my colleagues. They had no real reason to want Riley dead."

"You're convinced there's no strong motive for Quinn's death?" Sigrid asked with answering heat. "Fine! Makes no difference to me. My job doesn't change. Only, if you believe that, then you've got to believe there's an even stronger motive for *your* death. That poison was deliberately set there for one of you. Personally if it were me, I'd hope the poisoner had already got the one he wanted!"

Nauman glared at her, then turned and stalked from the tavern.

The gold-toothed waiter hurried over and helped Sigrid into her jacket with rough courtesy. "*Buenas noches, señora, y muchas gracias,*" he beamed as she added another bill to Nauman's for a tip, then crossed the saw-dust floor at a serene pace. There was dead silence as she passed the bar. Most of the men had been unaware of her presence until then. She saw no reason to hurry. This was not a well-frequented section of town at night; Nauman would be waiting on the sidewalk.

Instead she stepped outside just in time to see a cab pull away from the curb. The rearview window framed a halo of silver hair. Clinically Sigrid noted a small prick of regret that their evening had ended like this.

How odd!

9

Working late in his office, Captain McKinnon saw Sigrid pass his open door and called out to her.

She entered reluctantly, stopping just inside the door and pretending not to see his gesture toward a chair.

Captain McKinnon was built like a grizzled, over-grown teddy bear: rumpled looking and easygoing until faced with incompetence. Then his staff realized that the muscles on that large frame hadn't softened with paper-work, and that those sleepy brown eyes had noted every lapse up to and including the one they were being chewed out for right then.

In the past year Sigrid had often caught the captain looking at her with a puzzled expression as if he ex-pected something more from her, and it made her uneasy. Could he possibly have worked with her father? They would have been about the same age. Probably not, though; for whenever she met anyone who'd known her parents—blond, laughing Leif and dark, beautiful Anne—that person sooner or later commented on how different the daughter was from the parents.

Sigrid had built up no special myths about her father in her mind, but her mother never talked of his police work, and Sigrid would have liked to know what kind of officer he'd been—how competent, how dedicated, how involved. The old-timers on the force who actually re-membered Leif Harald were few, and they seldom con-nected her name to his. In any event, she was too reserved to approach them and ask for their memories.

For the thousandth time Sigrid wished she'd in-herited her father's happy congeniality or her mother's knack of immediate friendliness. She knew how stiff and cold she must still seem to her colleagues, but to be otherwise was impossible. Although she was no longer a tongue-tied child, a considerable shyness continued to numb her in social situations.

Here in the department some of the men still resented her promotion over them; some felt threatened; some ignored her completely. Yet even with the two or three like Detective Tildon, who respected her competence and accepted her presence among them, there was no easy give-and-take of camaraderie and laughter.

None of which bothered Sigrid Harald. Or so she thought.

Nevertheless, Captain McKinnon did make her uneasy, and she couldn't quite analyze the reason why. He was scrupulously fair and treated her the same as his other officers—piled on work and distributed praise and criticism with absolute impartiality. Yet always there was that vague air of expectation. Because she was female?

Efficiently she summarized for her superior the completion of the investigation into that doctor's knifing and outlined the situation at Vanderlyn College.

"Cohen's preliminary findings were on my desk just now. 'Respiratory paralysis and shock as a result of ingestion of potassium dichromate.' That's one of the chemicals from the print workshop, and anybody in the department could have got hold of it without being noticed."

"No A.P.B. out for that kid, what's his name?" McKinnon asked mildly.

"Harris, sir; Harley Harris. I didn't think it justified yet. I sent a man over to his home, and he reported that the parents seem cooperative. If Harris shows, they'll probably make him get in touch."

"What about that Hungarian janitor?"

"The same. Physically he could have done it. We think he had access to the closet key, and he was alone with the victim's coffee cup." She gave a brief description of how Szabo had carried the tray for Sandy Keppler.

"The girl couldn't have exposed that tray to more

potential poisoners if she'd sent it around Times Square,"
McKinnon said sourly. "Better have that Szabo in for a
thorough questioning just the same."

"His landlady said he hadn't been home since this
morning; I thought I'd try again later."

Her voice was cool and her gray eyes stony. Leif's
eyes, wondered McKinnon. Leif Harald's eyes had been
piercingly blue to match a blond Viking's build. His
daughter had his slender height, and yes, the shape of
the eyes was his; but the color, as well as her dark hair,
came from Anne.

McKinnon still remembered how he'd felt a year
ago upon her assignment to his department. To open her
folder and read Mrs. Leif Harald under the next-of-kin
heading had been an unexpected shock. When one of
Anne's photo essays had been nominated for a Pulitzer
a while back, he'd assumed that Harald was just a professional name by now, that she surely must have remarried. He should have known better.

He looked across his cluttered desk at the reserved
young woman who stood just inside his doorway without
nervousness, without fidgeting, until he would be done
with this interview and dismiss her. If she remembered
him even slightly, she'd given no hint of it.

And after all, she'd been very young—a thin solemn-
eyed little girl who'd clung to her mother's hand, bewildered by the ceremony; while he, McKinnon, had
been only another blue uniform with bright brass buttons, one of a dozen honor guards at her father's funeral.
Anne had refused to let him be more than that.

They had been such unlikely partners—McKinnon,
stolid, deliberate and motivated by logic; Leif Harald,
mercurial and intuitive. The combination had worked,
though, and had carried over into their off-duty social
life until that day in a dark hallway of a third-rate hotel,
where a killer had gone to earth behind one of those thin
doors. When it was over, the killer was dead, and the
dark bearlike man had walked out unmarked; but his
partner, the golden Viking, was carried out on a stretcher,

the blood already drying and turning black around those
bullet holes in his body.

"*Murderer!*" Anne had screamed. Had she filled the
girl with hate over the years? Was that what kept those
gray eyes so steady and noncommittal whenever they met
his?

McKinnon wrenched himself away from that night
and put the years behind him with a sigh. Better to keep
it all official, perhaps. Personalities complicated things.
If he had to take on a woman officer, Lieutenant Harald
seemed one of the best. At least he hadn't been stuck
with a sex bomb who could keep his staff room teetering
on the edge of an explosion. The loose, tailored pantsuits,
the dark hair skinned back into a knot at the nape of her
neck, the minimal makeup—hell! There were times like
tonight when she looked closer to forty than thirty. No
trouble on that score.

And yet it pained him to see Anne's daughter looking
so finely drawn.

"Not burning the candle at both ends, are you, Harald?" he asked, attempting a jocular note.

"Sir?"

"A joke. What I mean is, you're not working too
hard, are you? We're supposed to be using the pass-
along system, remember?"

Sigrid remembered. Difficult not to with the city
going deeper into the red every year. There had been
severe layoffs among personnel, and cutbacks had been
ordered everywhere. In an effort to reduce departmental
overtime, officers going off duty were encouraged to pass
their cases along to the officer on the next shift. The
procedure had indeed cut down on overtime, but no one
really liked it. "Pass along" meant losing your identifi-
cation with a case, your pride in a job well done when
you cracked it wide open. Sigrid sensed that McKinnon
didn't like it any more than she did, and others in the
bureau complained of feeling like pieceworkers on an
assembly line. Overtime dropped, but further compli-
ance was a sometime thing. Unless a situation was really

coming unraveled with a need to act quickly, many officers tried to hang onto the cases they'd begun until the next shift.

"This department is officially committed to eight-hour shifts, Harald, and it's nearly ten now."

"I had no intention of filing overtime," Sigrid said with the first hint of heat she'd allowed into her voice. "Anyhow, you're still here, sir."

"The privilege of rank," he said loftily.

There! That almost got one of her rare smiles. Inordinately pleased, he dismissed her with a wave. "No more work tonight, Lieutenant. Leave Szabo till tomorrow and that's an order."

Driving uptown, Sigrid was bemused. Burning the candle at both ends, indeed! As if she spent the nights dancing in chiffon until dawn. Had it been Duckett or Lyles, the two who most resented her presence in the department, she would have looked for the insult buried in the gibe. But McKinnon? No matter how she looked at that last exchange, there was only one conclusion: the captain had felt fatherly toward her. It was a novel idea.

And strangely warming. She could never remember getting that sort of reaction from a man. Her father's uncles had offered a kindly solicitude that arose more from duty than from choice. Looking back on it, Sigrid didn't blame them. All had possessed grandchildren of their own, and she knew—regretfully but objectively—that she had not been a lovable child. In formal greeting or departure she had given the ritual kisses that the family expected, but never had she hugged one of them impulsively. Too, on those long-ago Sunday afternoons she had been eclipsed whenever Cousin Hilda came over from her house just down the street.

Cousin Hilda had been plump and winsome with silver-blond curls and delft-blue eyes, and she had always elbowed Sigrid aside to hold Great-uncle Lars's hand on those walks to the zoo. Carelessly, lavishly, she bestowed kisses at the slightest provocation. The family pet. And the more demonstrative Hilda had been, the more touch-me-not Sigrid must have seemed.

Hilda had grown into a blithe young matron, still as plump and merry as in childhood. Married to an insurance broker or a C.P.A.—Sigrid could never remember which—she now lived in Port Jefferson out on Long Island with a family of plump and merry children. Four of them, the last time Sigrid heard.

While I've grown into a dried-up old maid, she told herself. She peered through the windshield, momentarily distracted from her thoughts by a dilemma familiar to all drivers: the misty night air had deposited enough moisture on the glass to bead up soot and grime and to make seeing difficult, but was it really misting enough to wash all the dirt away if she turned on the wipers? The windshield was now so obscured that further debate became academic. She pushed the washer button and wipers simultaneously, and one feeble stream of water jetted up. Just enough to make a complete smear when the blades swished back and forth.

I remember to get gas, she told herself savagely, I remember to check the oil and the transmission fluid, so why the hell can't I remember to keep the washer bottle filled?

And no, dammit, it was *not* misting enough to clean the glass.

Briefly she wondered if Cousin Hilda ever had these mundane automotive aggravations, or did acquiring a C.P.A. husband free you from that?

Which brought a rueful smile to her lips, because however much she might wish she were less stiff in social situations, no way did she envy Cousin Hilda's life. She was chagrined by the circuitous path her thoughts had taken, all because Captain McKinnon had given her a couple of casual fatherly words in passing.

The mist thickened into a slow drizzle, and now the wipers managed to clear the windshield. She enjoyed driving through the streets at night. Especially in midtown when she was in no hurry to get home. Traffic had

begun to pick up as movies and theaters emptied out
onto the sidewalks. There were more cabs, buses and
private cars and knots of people descending into the
subway. Few people cared to go down alone at night
anymore, which was a shame. Violence or the fear of
violence kept so many from utilizing fully the only sensible way of getting around the five boroughs; but violence was a fact of life, and it was futile to feel that spasm
of anger.

"Do what you can and don't let the rest eat on you."
All rookies got that lecture. Good advice. If you could
follow it during your shift, pass everything along when
you left and keep your eyes averted when you were off
duty, there would be fewer policemen nursing ulcers.
As it was, every precinct house in the city could furnish
enough antacid remedies to stock a small drugstore.

A smell compounded of gasoline fumes, buttered
popcorn and wet pavement slid in through her slightly
opened window as she stopped for a red light at Times
Square. The drizzle was starting to take itself seriously;
might almost be called a true rain; yet the boy and girl
who passed dreamily in front of her car were oblivious
to it, to the changed lights, to everything except each
other.

Sigrid drove on automatically, her mind only half-
aware of the mechanics of driving. Without noticing where
her thoughts had drifted, she found herself going over
the earlier part of the evening as she contrasted Captain
McKinnon's kindly air of solidity with Oscar Nauman's
brusqueness.

Nauman was older than McKinnon as calendars run;
but there was a curiously youthful, unfinished quality
about the artist. He was a mature man, no little-boy-not-
grown-up, yet he had retained an indefinable youthful
quality. As if he were still in a state of becoming. As if
the world still held new surprises, new possibilities, after
all these years.

Probably the artistic temperament, Sigrid thought

scornfully; but a sudden impulse made her head the car crosstown toward her mother's apartment.

She told herself it was time to anyhow. Whenever Anne was out of town, Sigrid stopped by to pick up mail and to make sure everything was okay. It was her duty, she told herself firmly, and curiosity about what Oscar Nauman had looked like fifteen years ago had nothing to do with it.

10

Her mother's current apartment was in one of the newer high-rises overlooking the Hudson River. Some women shift furniture; Anne Harald kept all the same pieces of furniture in approximately the same positions and restlessly shifted apartments instead. Her friends had long since learned to enter her new telephone and street numbers in their address books in light, easily erased pencil. Anne had inhabited Manhattan Island from the Battery to Harlem. She'd even crossed the East River once and tried Brooklyn Heights, but that was a short-lived experiment. Shorter still had been a sojourn in Connecticut. The U-Haul rental truck had deposited Anne and her chattels in a picturesquely rustic cottage on a Tuesday afternoon. An identical truck had carted everything back to Manhattan the following Friday morning.

These frequent moves had been so much a part of Sigrid's childhood that she no longer recalled that they had begun immediately after Leif's funeral. By now it was just another quirk of Anne's personality; easier to shrug one's shoulders and accept it than to try to understand.

This year's building was all glass and steel, its ground floor as impersonal as a bank and quite bare except for the slight softening effect of low fern-filled planters along the front walls, a colorful mosaic floor and a few backless leather benches clumped together in the center of the lobby. At the rear were elevators and banked mailboxes. The whole place was as brightly lit as an all-night diner and even less inviting, but it was virtually mugger-proof.

To compensate for the lack of doorman, tenants could inspect everything behind those floor-to-ceiling glass walls before unlocking the street door and letting themselves in, and there were no shadowy culs-de-sac where a rapist could lurk undetected.

Closed-circuit televisions on the main door and in the elevator videotaped everyone coming or going, and it was useless to tell her mother that the tapes probably weren't checked unless a tenant actually got mugged. Anne was convinced that a watchman or somebody monitored them, and unless she were in a tearing hurry, she always blew kisses to the cameras or thumbed her nose or modeled a new dress.

"They must get so bored just watching people galumph in and out as if they're going to their own funerals," she would say.

Whenever her mother was brightening up a hypothetical watchman's day, Sigrid would stand to the far side of the elevator and pretend not to know her.

It was raining briskly when Sigrid slipped inside the lobby and paused long enough to empty Anne's mailbox. Some of the letters had been forwarded through five or six addresses. She took a self-service elevator to the eighteenth floor and let herself into a front apartment.

Anne Harald's image stood just inside the vestibule with arms outstretched. A fellow photographer had cleverly matched front and back views, blown them up, then laminated them together into a rigid sheet of acrylic to form a life-sized cutout doll who welcomed her visitors the way Anne welcomed life—with open arms; dimples flashing; short hair an exuberance of dark curls; her slender body still petite and shapely at fifty.

Anne herself used the thing as a hat stand, draping it in scarves, light meters and paraphernalia cases, but it was too lifelike for Sigrid's taste. She always hurried past it when making her tours of inspection.

Things were normal that evening. Nothing dramatic

like burst water pipes or signs of forced entry, although
a stranger might have had difficulty distinguishing between a burglar's ransacking and Anne's normal going-
away clutter. Every drawer was slightly ajar, and every
surface overflowed. Film cartridges were jumbled in with
sliding piles of professional journals, unanswered letters,
discarded panty hose, airline itineraries and butt-filled
ashtrays. Anne's departures were perennially hurried.
Schedules always surprised her.

"The plane leaves at *noon*?" she'd wail. "But it's
eleven now! Who's got a car? Where's my coat? My
camera bags?"

Some people found her disorganized, chaotic air
appealing. Sigrid preferred order and calm; but because
she'd lived apart from her mother since college, it was
not a source of friction any longer. Now they could look
at each other fondly—if somewhat quizzically—across
the generation gap.

Like many untidy people, Anne Harald kept surprisingly meticulous records. Five large steel file cabinets followed in her wake wherever she moved. Couches,
tables, bric-a-brac and rugs had become battered and
shabby from occupying haphazard spaces on those do-it-
yourself moves organized and executed by the youthful
neophyte photographers who clustered around Anne; but
the file cabinets were always the last on and first off those
rental trucks. Admittedly Anne's filing system was pe-
culiarly her own and not always logical; but sooner or
later she could lay her hands on any of her negatives, or
her magazine and newspaper articles from the last twenty-
five years.

Under the *S*'s was a file with Sigrid's name on it,
begun in her fifth year because Anne had obtained and
then managed to misplace three separate copies of her
daughter's birth certificate, and the kindergarten wouldn't
enter Sigrid without proof that she'd been born the proper
number of years before. The folder still contained Sigrid's
immunization and dental records and the pediatrician's

careful listing of childhood diseases, report cards and—though Anne always denied being sentimental—every Mother's Day card Sigrid had ever labored over in grade school and all her letters from boarding school and college, which strangely touched Sigrid the first time she had stumbled upon her folder.

She located the old *Life* article on her first try, pulled it out and started to close the drawer when another folder nearer the front caught her eye.

It was labeled simply "Leif", and it was not very thick. Inside were a couple of letters addressed to Miss Anne Lattimore in her father's masculine scrawl, a birth certificate, diplomas, a driver's license, a medal and its accompanying posthumous citation, some police-department forms dealing with death benefits and a handful of pictures.

Sigrid had seen most of the pictures before but not in several years. She had difficulty locating her father in a group-graduation pose, one skinhead rookie out of a whole class of uniformed look-alikes. There was a formal studio portrait—how very young he looked—and a close-up of herself at six months, sitting on his lap, wearing his patrolman's hat and gnawing on the handle of his service pistol.

In the last picture he was as she could just barely remember him: laughing directly into the camera, his fair hair slicked back, tall and handsome and utterly self-assured. A man's hand rested on his shoulder, and a closer look revealed that someone had been cropped from the picture. Odd. Idly she wondered who it was, and why he'd been cut away. Along the right border was a date and in her mother's hasty script the words: "First day in plain clothes."

Two months before he'd been gunned down.

It was disorienting to look at the date and suddenly realize that she was now older than he had been. Somehow one never expects to grow older than one's parents. It upset life's natural order. Then she remembered the

time when she was still in uniform and had been sent
to tell an elderly mother that her son had been killed
in a car wreck that evening. The old woman had just
stared at her numbly, shaking her head over and over
in mute denial that finally came out in soft bewildered
cries, "But he isn't old enough. He's not old enough
to die."

Sigrid knew it must feel much more unnatural to
outlive a child than a parent; nevertheless, she gave a
final uneasy glance at her father's unlined face before
replacing the folder and closing the drawer. The *Life*
article she kept out to take back to her own apartment,
where she could relax finally with a bourbon and cola,
her one southern mannerism.

As she moved through the apartment switching off
lights, Sigrid was suddenly alerted to a furtive noise at
the front door. Adrenaline flowing, but without panic,
she quickly doused the remaining lights and positioned
herself behind it. Another soft click and it opened slowly.
Light from the hallway spilled in along with a case of
some sort. A figure followed, someone who carried a
small penlight that flashed along the floor and walls and
hesitated on the Anne-figure hat rack.

Moving to catch him off balance, Sigrid yanked the
door all the way back.

"That's far enough!" she told the dark figure silhou-
etted in the bright doorway. "Hands on the wall, mister,
feet spread. *Now!*"

The penlight jerked across her face, touched on
the gun she held in her right hand. There was a sharp
intake of breath, then the penlight wavered and slipped
to the floor from limp fingers. The man himself followed close behind, crumpling softly, almost noise-
lessly.

Sigrid had never had anyone faint on her before.
Bemused, she switched on the lights again, pulled the
man all the way across the threshold, then closed the
door and turned to examine her catch.

Male Caucasian, she thought, automatically falling

into official-report jargon. Age? Late thirties. Hair (what there was of it) a sandy brown, almost no gray. Long on the sides and probably usually brushed forward to augment a hairline that had receded to the dome of his head. Eyes closed now, of course. Well nourished but not actually fat. He was dressed rather like someone out for a day of elephant hunting in the Serengeti: wide-brimmed canvas hat, rumpled khaki safari suit, open-necked shirt and leopard-print silk scarf. Instead of boots he wore fawn-colored suede shoes with thick crepe soles.

Since he wasn't actually carrying an elephant gun, Sigrid put her own .38 away and slipped her hand inside his breast pocket. She came out with a wallet, an airline folder and a passport. Passport and wallet indicated that the man was Roman Tramegra, age forty-two. According to the ticket stubs in his Alitalia folder, his flight had arrived at Kennedy International an hour or so earlier; but the whole trip had orginated with a flight from Sardinia.

Which came very near to explaining everything. Her mother was at last report in Italy on assignment for *Eyewitness*. The newsmagazine planned to devote a fall issue to the state of worldwide violence and terrorism, and Anne and two other free-lance journalists were gathering background material and local color on how kidnapping had become almost a cottage industry in Italy.

Another of Anne's displaced persons, and she had just terrified him into fainting.

Ever since Sigrid could remember, an odd assortment of characters had wandered in and out of her mother's life. Anne attracted them the way some people attract stray dogs and cats; and just as an animal lover always manages to find good homes for his waifs, Anne was equally successful at finding homes or jobs or sanctuary of some sort for her strays. Sigrid wondered what category Roman Tramegra would fall into.

She rolled him onto a small Turkestan rug and dragged

it across the vinyl-tile floor to a couch in the living room. There she shoved aside a couple of Anne's geopolitical maps, hoisted him onto the couch and slid cushions under his feet. Returning from the bathroom with a cold cloth for his forehead, she found him blinking heavy-lidded blue eyes in her direction.

"Oh, good, you're awake," she said. "Can I get you something? Coffee, tea or bourbon?"

"Don't bother. You've done quite enough already," he said coldly, sitting up and adjusting the leopard-print scarf at the neck of his shirt. His voice was unexpectedly deep, a bit pompous and with more than a touch of affronted dignity.

"Look," Sigrid told him, "I do apologize for what happened. My mother didn't tell me she was lending the apartment, and I thought you'd picked the lock. I'm sorry."

He smoothed the long piece of side hair carefully into place across the top of his head. "She said you were a policewoman, so I *quite* understand your reaction. Please *don't* give it another thought. My fault for not ringing the doorbell first. Still it never occurred to me that anyone was inside. Anne said the place was here going idle, and I thought—" He took a deep breath and gave her an abashed smile, which made him look more human. "I'm simply chattering, aren't I? I always talk too much when I've been upset. Reaction, I expect. You mentioned tea. I *do* hope it's souchong."

Sigrid shook her head. "Lipton."

"Loose?" he asked, clutching at straws.

"Sorry, only tea bags, I'm afraid," Sigrid said gravely, privately amused rather than insulted by the man's air of having landed among savages.

There was a brief internal struggle, then he shrugged his shoulders in a what-more-can-one-expect gesture of resignation. "Tea bags will be fine."

As Sigrid started for the kitchen, he exclaimed, "How careless of me! I almost forgot I have a letter for you." He fumbled in his breast pocket. "Gone! My wallet—"

"There on the coffee table," she said; and as he drew himself up, she said defensively, "For all I knew, you could have been a thief."

"And you thought I might have been carrying my own Wanted Poster, Miss Harald?" he said icily. Then in another of his abrupt about-faces, he asked curiously, "Do they?"

Sigrid was caught off guard. "Do who what?"

"Thieves. Do they ever carry clippings of their exploits? You know: 'Tiffany's robbed of half a million in diamonds during daring morning theft.' Things of that nature." He had found the letter in his wallet and handed it to her as he waited for her answer.

"I really don't know," she said nonplussed. "I suppose it's possible, but I've never heard of it. I've never worked Burglary, though."

"I may do a detective novel. I'm a writer, you see," he confided, padding down the hall behind her as she headed for the kitchen. "I could have the criminal keep a scrapbook with newspaper clippings of all his nefarious deeds, and after he was caught, there would be a marvelous denouement with my detective realizing that he hadn't known *half* the crimes my gangster had committed. He'd be simply *flabbergasted!*"

Tramegra beamed at her. "You'll probably find me a complete nuisance before I've finished, Miss Harald, but I warn you I'm going to pick your brain for technical details. They're very important in a book. Attention to detail is what separates the careful writer from the hack, you know."

His accent was an amalgam of cinema British, Boston Yankee, and American Midwest, and he was still burbling as Sigrid pointed him in the direction of the bathroom to freshen up.

In the kitchen she filled the kettle, unearthed a seldom used teapot, rinsed out the dust and put in two

tea bags, their tagged strings dangling over the edge.
As she waited for the water to boil, she read Anne's
letter:

> *Cagliari, April 12*
>
> *Siga, dear,*
>   *Sorry not to have written before. Italy's
> got weird. The kidnappings would be funny if
> none of them were violent. Can you believe that
> a carabiniere's wife was held for $110 last week?
> None of us go anywhere alone, and we dress
> and look like retired schoolteachers without a
> soul in the world to pay even a $10 ransom.*

Sigrid paused for a moment to imagine what her
mother's idea of a retired schoolteacher would be. She
doubted Anne could make herself look that dowdy. Then
back to the letter:

> *But I'll write you all about it another time
> because this is supposed to be introducing Ro-
> man Tramegra. I've told him he can use my
> place while I'm gone. That'll save you having
> to come over. Be nice to him. He's had a very
> difficult time lately—someone rooked him of his
> money, and he doesn't want to talk about it.
> Not that you would ask, I know, but you do
> have a way of looking at people until they feel
> so guilty that they start babbling too much.*
>   *There, you see? You've even got me doing
> it long-distance.*
>   *Anyhow, Romey's a dear, sweet man. And
> he does need a place to stay while he researches
> his novel—something to do with a man who
> falls in love with a holographic image or some-
> thing like that. (He seemed to think I'd know
> how holograms work just because I'm a pho-
> tographer. When I don't even know how a reflex
> camera works!)*

*See you sometime next month. Shall I bring
you a sheepskin rug?*

                                        *Love,
                                        mother*

The kettle whistled stridently. Sigrid filled the teapot, added sugar and a jar of nondairy creamer to the
mug and spoon already on the tray and carried it into
the living room.

Tramegra had exchanged his jacket and scarf for a
dark brown cardigan. Again Sigrid noted a softness about
him, though he couldn't be called fat. An impression of
fragile bones beneath a covering of soft flesh. Then she
remembered a large, soft Persian cat her southern grandmother had owned—that was what Roman Tramegra
reminded her of—a large, soft, pampered cat, amiable,
but always with a slight reserve of dignity behind the
amiability.

He moved aside a bowl of dead flowers and gathered
up a handful of odds and ends to clear a space on the
coffee table for the tray Sigrid carried.

"Ah, tea," he exclaimed. "How welcome it is! And
you mustn't apologize for the imitation cream. No one
could produce fresh milk on such short notice." Still
there was an involuntary lift of his eyebrow when he
noticed the mug instead of a china cup and saucer, as
if she really might make apology for that lapse. Manners triumphed, however, and he said, "Aren't you
joining me?"

"Sorry," she said, glancing at her watch. It was after
eleven. "This has been a long day. The guest room's
second on the left there; I think mother keeps its linens
in the bottom bureau drawer."

They both looked around the big messy living area.
Sigrid supposed she should make some sort of effort, but
she was too tired. Instead she gathered up her jacket,
purse and the *Life* folder. "If you can't find anything,
just root around," she advised him. "And if you need
me, I'm in the phone book."

"Oh, I'm sure I'll manage," he said, pouring his tea. "All this really needs is a good vacuuming." He looked again at the clutter—at the heaps of newspapers and magazines piled beside couches and chairs and under tables, at the moldy coffee mugs, ashtrays and stray pieces of feminine apparel.

"Or maybe a shovel," Sigrid heard him amend as she let herself out.

11

From infancy Sigrid had known puzzled looks from her mother's friends. Sooner or later would be murmured the inevitable, "She certainly doesn't take after you or Leif, does she?"

The comparisons didn't hurt less for being voiced in soft southern accents as Sigrid discovered the Christmas Anne was delayed by an assignment in the Philippines. Grandmother Lattimore had come up from North Carolina to keep Sigrid company when she came home from boarding school, thirteen years old and at her very gawkiest.

Mrs. Lattimore had raised three feminine belles, and she was at a loss with this Yankee granddaughter. She had brought Sigrid a Christmas dress of red velvet and white lace, but even she immediately saw how inappropriate such a dress would be on a child all arms and legs. Sigrid was already two inches taller than her grandmother. Her hair was dark like Anne's, but its absolute straightness came from Leif, and it was so silky fine that it frizzed when Mrs. Lattimore tried to curl it.

"You've got a lot of things about you like your mama and daddy, honey," the woman had sighed, "only you just went and put them together differently. Well, I guess it doesn't really matter. They say you're going to be real intelligent. That's nice." Her voice had been dubious; then more briskly she'd added, "You're still not grown up yet, and if you cultivate a pleasant personality, why, you'll do just fine! Look at your Cousin Lunette—plain as an old board fence, and she was the most popular girl of her year. Eight marriage proposals before she was twenty, and she had those squinchy little eyes from the

Howard side of her family. At least yours are nice and wide, honey. All you need to do is learn to use them."

Anne had always talked about the "marvelous planes" of her face; but after Grandmother Lattimore's blunt assessment Sigrid had gone into the bathroom, locked the door and studied herself feature by feature, angrily brushing away the tears that welled up in her clear gray eyes. Coldly she noted that her face wasn't actually repulsive, and that grandmother was right. Her eyes probably were her best feature. They would have to suffice.

Since then Sigrid had stopped looking in mirrors except to be sure everything hung together decently. Once and for all on that thirteenth Christmas she had decided—and accepted the fact—that she was homely and ungraceful, and it had never occurred to her that she might have changed. Or that there were standards of beauty other than her grandmother's stereotype.

She had no idea how stunning she could look when alone in the evenings, her dark hair loose, and robed in one of the exotic djellabas or caftans that Anne kept sending from all over the world. Tonight's was a deep wine red with sleeves and hem widely banded by rich embroidery interspersed with crystal beads and tiny mirrors no larger than a thumbnail.

When it arrived last Christmas Sigrid had sighed at her mother's frivolous taste, and she'd scowled at her reflection upon trying it on—peacock feathers on a crow, she'd thought—but by now habit and familiarity had made it as unremarkable as gray flannel. Only gray flannel didn't complement her skin as did the robe. She was a barbaric splash of color as she curled up on her white linen couch to read the old *Life* article, and the lamplight did interesting things to the hollows of her cheeks and eyes as she concentrated on the magazine.

The article on modern American artists had been her mother's first important assignment with a major magazine, and her success with it had led to other plums. Perhaps anyone could have photographed the artworks as cleanly, but the Anne Harald touch lay in the way her camera caught each artist's personality and philosophy more openly than usual as the subjects responded to the woman behind the lens.

Seven lesser luminaries shared one double spread, but Oscar Nauman had been one of five artists who had double pages to themselves. There he was in what Sigrid now recognized as a characteristic pose: his lean frame carelessly sprawled in a chair, but both hands gesturing in an inward curve as he strove to make his point. One could almost feel the energy and intensity contained in that gesture.

The straightforward captions beneath each picture served mainly to identify the subject; but in the accompanying four-page essay Riley Quinn's prose was lucid and his positions were well-argued. Sigrid had never been able to get past what she regarded as the paradoxes and put-ons of modern art, but Quinn's style was vivid and easy to follow. Although aggressively opinionated, he had made his points confidently and logically and had marshaled excellent concrete examples to back up his statements.

One would need a strong ego and an even stronger grounding in modernism to refute him or beat him in his own area, and Sigrid began to understand how an artist might fear for his reputation if Riley Quinn turned thumbs down on his work.

As Quinn had planned to do to Piers Leyden? With relish, if one could believe all accounts.

One small dose of innocent-looking orange crystals, and Leyden could subvert Quinn's book and take possession of Quinn's beautiful wife.

Nauman had made it sound as if the affair with Leyden were of no importance, yet even drunk and passed out, Doris Quinn had been stunning. Or wasn't Oscar Nauman impressed by bosomy blondes?

Sigrid turned back to his photograph and idly wondered what type of woman he *did* prefer. Silver hair notwithstanding, she rather doubted if there had been a lessening of his vitality in that particular area any more than in his art. Those hands, for instance . . . sturdy, square-shaped workman's hands, powerful enough to shape and mold yet capable of delicacy and precision. Of gentle, lyrical touch . . .

Sigrid sat bolt upright and slammed the folder shut, her cheeks suddenly stained by a blush more crimson than her exotic robe. Oscar Nauman was old enough to be her father!

Dismayed at herself, she went into the kitchen to make a cup of hot chocolate; and while the milk heated, she spilled the little squares of red paper onto her white counter top and began sorting the tones. The milk boiled over, was turned off and grew cold as she struggled with the problem of arranging the squares in nine equal steps. The girl student had been right: twelve steps *were* rather easy. But nine evaded her.

She poured the curdled milk down the drain and washed the pan, then switched off all the lights and went to bed.

And found herself right back at square one, wondering if Oscar Nauman slept alone tonight.

What the devil had got into her?

She buried her head under a pillow, blocked out every undisciplined thought and put herself firmly to sleep by a concentrated listing of all fifty states in alphabetical order.

12

Although not a morning person, Sigrid usually awoke before her alarm went off, so when a ringing penetrated her sleep next morning, her first response as she fumbled for the cutoff button was a drowsy surprise that she'd overslept.

The ringing continued. Was cataloged as doorbell, not clock.

Sigrid groped for her robe and stumbled barefooted through her apartment to the door, then after a startled glance through the peephole, undid the latch.

Upon her threshold stood Oscar Nauman, indecently wide awake and as bright as the dawn sunlight edging in through her east windows. Thick white hair still damp from his morning shower, freshly shaven and smelling of a good German cologne, he wore dark chinos and a pale blue turtleneck shirt; he also looked disgustingly like a man who'd just played two vigorous sets of tennis or jogged five miles. Sigrid's first impulse was to close the door again immediately and go back to bed.

"Do you know what time it is?" she asked crossly.

He consulted a thin gold watch. "Five-thirty-eight. I assume you have to be at work by seven, so that leaves us an hour for a nice leisurely breakfast." He waved a small grocery bag. "I brought jam and eggs for a strawberry omelet."

The idea of eggs that early in the morning—to say nothing of eggs with jam on them—was so repulsive that Sigrid stepped back involuntarily.

Nauman interpreted that as an invitation and breezed past her toward the kitchen. Sigrid followed, protesting,

"I don't have to check in till eight, and I *never* eat break-fast."

"*That* I can believe," he said, rummaging in her refrigerator. He'd never seen one so bare in a woman's kitchen. The top shelf held orange juice, a pound can of coffee and a quart of milk that would be sour by tomorrow. There were a couple of cheeses, a stick of butter, a loaf of whole-wheat bread, peanut butter, mayonnaise, three brown bananas, and a head of wilted lettuce turning brown at the stalk. Nothing more.

Incredulously he opened cupboard doors and found a toaster, two saucepans, one skillet, a half-dozen cans of soup, cocoa mix, three cans of tuna, and a box of crackers. Salt, pepper, and sugar completed her staples.

"Soup's all you ever cook?"

"And grilled cheese. That's a balanced enough meal. I suppose you fix yourself a four-course dinner every night?"

"What happens when someone drops in for a meal?" he asked, genuinely curious.

"No one with any manners 'drops in,' " Sigrid said acidly. "They wait for an invitation, and then I take them to a proper restaurant." She picked up a percolator from the counter behind him, rinsed it and filled it with cold water, then measured coffee into the basket. Morning sunlight caught the shiny beads and mirrors of her robe so that with every movement of her slender arms and hands, tiny rainbows of prismed sunlight flashed and coruscated on the surfaces all around her.

Nauman was enchanted. His artist's eyes moved from the fugitive, darting colors to their source, then widened as he really saw her: narrow feet bare on the tile floor, the boy-slim body made graceful by the clinging red robe, the tilt of her head that sent long dark hair swinging as she plugged in the percolator.

In an exuberance of delight at the picture she made, he turned her to him, lifted her chin with his strong fingers, and placed an impromptu kiss on her startled lips.

He'd meant nothing more serious than his usual homage to unexpected beauty; but as she tried to pull away, something made him tighten his hold and kiss her again. She wrenched herself from his arms, gray eyes blazing with anger as she searched for the cutting insult.

"*You*—You must be at least sixty!"

"Which still makes me thirty years younger than you!" he retorted. The thought made him grin unrepentantly. "Never kissed an older woman before, but it's an experience worth repeating."

She glared at him speechless as he moved toward her purposefully, then fled from the sunlit kitchen, taking all the rainbows with her. A moment later and her bedroom door banged shut. Thoughtfully Nauman broke eggs into a bowl and began beating them with a fork.

She doesn't know she's a woman, he decided at last, and found that the thought both disturbed and intrigued him.

Sigrid leaned against her closed door and drew a deep steadying breath as the clink of metal upon glass reached her ears. Mind and reason warred with unfamiliar, muddled emotions as she stripped and headed for her bath. She turned the shower on full, and jets of water streamed down upon her body until the convulsive turmoil was sluiced away, and her equanimity was almost restored. Then the bathroom door opened, and she heard Nauman's voice above the water.

"Your coffee, Lieutenant."

"Will you get the hell out of here?" she cried angrily.

He was gone when she turned off the water and peered around the curtain, but she snapped the door bolt anyhow before toweling herself dry.

The coffee that he'd left on the lavatory was more welcome than she wanted to admit, and she took a big swallow, then tackled her damp hair. A few minutes sufficed to plait it into a thick braid and secure it at the nape of her neck, and usually she didn't bother to wipe off the steam-fogged mirror. Today she polished it clear and examined herself closely to make sure every hair was pinned in place. She noticed that her cheeks were flushed an unaccustomed pink and splashed cold water on them until the color subsided.

Another prudent look from the doorway revealed that her bedroom was also empty, so Sigrid crossed the fern-green carpet to her open closet. Normally she would have worn the next dark pantsuit in line, a dull gray, with another white silk shirt like yesterday's; but nothing was normal this morning, and she flipped past it, finding nothing in her closet to fit her unsettled mood until she reached the far end of the rack where she kept what she called her Carolina wardrobe.

From time out of mind all Lattimore females (if one could believe her grandmother) had been captivating fillies who left a trail of broken hearts behind them on their single-minded trek to the altar. All had made brilliant matches to the most eligible bachelors of their seasons, and it was bad taste for Sigrid to remark on the ones that had ended in divorce. After all, what sort of marriage did *she* expect to make? Such an unfeminine career, police work. Interesting, no doubt, but didn't one have to guard against becoming coarsened? Thus, Grandmother Lattimore.

Over the years Sigrid had found it easier to wear clothes of Anne's choosing for her annual duty visit south than to listen to her Grandmother Lattimore's complaints that she really wasn't trying.

Most of the clothes were too bright or too fussy for Sigrid's taste, but she paused at one that wasn't completely objectionable: a brushed cotton suit of soft moss-green and a cowl-necked silk shell in rich jewel tones of purples and blues. Even Grandmother Lattimore had approved of the way she looked in that one. But the only shoes that went with the outfit were frivolous green sling-back heels, and the matching bag could barely accommodate a wallet and lace handkerchief; there was certainly no room in it for a regulation pistol, badge and note pad.

All of which brought her to her senses with a grim

smile. Dithering over clothes as if Oscar Nauman were
Rhett Butler and she Scarlett O'Hara instead of a New
York cop! As if ugly ducklings really could become swans.
What had got into her?

Without pausing to analyze the question, Sigrid
flipped back to the shapeless gray pantsuit and dressed
with rapid efficiency. Her chin was high, and all her
defenses were in place when she emerged from her
bedroom.

To find him gone.

Only dirty dishes in her sink, and a note on the
counter to advise that he'd eaten his breakfast with relish,
thank you, and hers was in the oven. She opened the
oven door and took out a tender omelet and buttered
toast, still warm on a plate.

Toast, yes, she thought, but the eggs are going down
the garbage disposal.

Curiosity made her try a bite.

It was delicious.

Bemused, she poured herself another cup of coffee
and perched on a step stool to eat the whole thing. Anchovies on her steak last night. And now jam with eggs.

To cap it all, the little squares of red that she'd been
trying to puzzle out last night lay in perfect alignment
on the counter—from the darkest red to the lightest pink
in nine even steps.

Damn the man!

13

Across town Andrea Ross was—like Sigrid—deliberating carefully over her choice of clothes but with a difference. Impractical shoes were very much a part of the picture she wanted to create. She was going to stage a deliberate and full-fledged retreat into femininity, and the morning sunlight was an innocent conspirator. It promised a spring day warm enough for shoes that were nothing more than delicate straps of braided straw and matched a straw-colored gathered skirt that fluttered softly around her legs. She topped the cotton skirt with a heavily embroidered Mexican peon shirt and studied the total effect in her mirror.

Getting there.

Next she skillfully manipulated a styling wand to transform her sensible short brown hair into a crown of ringlets, then made up her eyes to look as wide and appealing as a fawn's. A faint touch of blusher to her cheeks and another critical examination of her reflection.

Perfect!

She looked cool and poised enough to deliver scholarly lectures yet soft and womanly. Not helpless exactly but with no hard career edges showing. No single-minded ambitions, either, and certainly no vengeful thoughts.

Must watch the lips though, she decided, knowing that her lips looked too determined in repose, her eyes too shrewd.

Think soft, she told herself.

But her thoughts kept slipping away to the raise a promotion would mean. The grueling debts of her postgraduate years were almost repaid. There was beginning to be enough money for clothes, a decent apartment, books. The promotion she had expected—had *earned*, damn it—would have meant enough at last to spend a summer in France. As a true art lover, not a penny-pinching student. A summer to lie in fields of red poppies if she wished and drink in the soaring lines of Chartres Cathedral until that abiding thirst for perfection, unsatisfied since childhood, was finally slaked. She wanted to experience at last a direct response to what she saw with no worries of dates, theories or the pressures of a doctoral dissertation to come between herself and the art.

She had yearned for such a summer with an almost physical ache, and Riley Quinn had nearly cheated her of it for another few years by passing her over for Jake Saxer. As she remembered the blind fury she'd felt last week when she'd heard that Saxer had been recommended for promotion, Andrea Ross caught sight of her reflection in the mirror and was chilled by its granite grimness.

Think *soft*, she warned herself and tried to remember how innocence smiled.

In the two-family brick house he owned within walking distance of the university, Professor Albert Simpson's tea and toast grew cold as he contemplated promotion to deputy chairman. Although he did not possess Riley Quinn's outside reputation, he *was* the most senior art historian, and no one questioned his command of his subject.

No one respected it, either, he told himself wryly. No one except young Wade. On the other hand, he had no enemies; no one disliked him strongly enough to vote against him, so the balloting should be a mere formality. The younger historians would probably look upon his tenure in the chair as a caretaker regime, soon to be ended by his retirement. It would give them time to square off at each other for a real battle when he stepped down.

The last time that chair had been vacant, they'd

offered it to him first; but he'd turned it down, not wanting the encumbrances of administrative duties that would take him away from the classroom and eat into his precious research time. His refusal had opened up a scramble among the other younger historians, and Riley Quinn had emerged victorious—Quinn, who'd begun by using the title to further his extracurricular career; who had never neglected an opportunity to sneer at the man whose stepping aside had made it possible for him to hold that title; and who had over the years finally grown so arrogant that he'd actually commandeered a classroom teacher, Jake Saxer, to be his personal researcher for the latest of those books he churned out. Catchpenny, simplified popularizations of the passing art scene. As if what passed for art today needed further simplification!

Professor Simpson added another spoonful of sugar to his tea and sipped meditatively. It was stone-cold now, but that was so usual he barely noticed.

At most he was only four years from retirement, and in all the previous years he'd truly never desired a titled position or rank over his peers; but Quinn had shown an advantage to the title that hadn't occurred to him before; and now that it was to be offered to him again, he would take it this time. Not that he would abuse it as Riley Quinn had. David Wade had too much character to be used as Quinn had used that fawning toad Saxer. But as a colleague—a collaborator—as the son he'd never had. Somehow he would use his newly acquired power to keep Wade here. At last his book would be finished.

He reached for the telephone and dialed Wade's number from memory. When there was no answer, he consulted the directory for a different number, then smiled indulgently at the appetites of youth as Sandy Keppler's lilting voice said, "It's for you, darling."

Sandy closed the bathroom door with an indulgent smile of her own. She'd never seen David so embarrassed before.

And it's rather sweet when you think about it, she

told herself, that he cares enough for your reputation to stammer out some corny explanation about coming over here for breakfast. ("She makes terrific French toast, sir," she'd heard him say as she was leaving the room.)

As if Professor Simpson, who knew all about the dissipations of classical Rome, would be shocked by a simple bedding down before marriage. David was such an innocent about some things.

She brushed her long yellow hair vigorously, touched her lips with pink lipstick and added a hint of blue shadow to her eyelids.

The murmur of David's voice still sounded, so she rinsed the sink, straightened towels, capped the toothpaste and uncapped his after-shave lotion for a quick whiff of spicy fragrance. So bound up in memories of their most intimate moments was that aroma that she'd once gone weak-kneed when she smelled it on a stranger on a crowded bus.

Tenderly she tucked the little bottle back into the medicine cabinet and went out to rejoin her now pensive lover.

"What did he want?" she asked as she passed him maple syrup and stirred cream into his coffee.

"I'm not really sure," said David. His eyes were puzzled behind his wire-rimmed glasses. He lifted a forkful of French toast, then returned it to his plate. "You know how he always goes off on tangents?"

Sandy nodded.

"He said the apartment on the top floor of his house has an extra bedroom that could be used as a study. He also said his present tenant doesn't have a lease."

"He's offering you an apartment?" she asked, perplexed.

"Us. You and me. Cheap."

"Just how cheap?" Sandy asked, knowing to a penny how far her salary would stretch. Her mouth dropped when he told her. "That's practically free, David! And it's only two blocks from school. No bus or subway fare!" She jumped up and hugged him exuberantly.

"It's charity," David said ominously, pulling away.

"No, it *isn't*! Don't you see? It's worth it to him to have your help organizing that mountain of notes for his book. It would be an equal exchange. Free rent instead of salary. Isn't that what *quid pro quo* means? And best of all, we wouldn't have to go to Idaho while you're finishing your dissertation."

Her voice had hit a strident tone he'd never heard.

"You really *don't* want to leave New York, do you?" he asked, frowning as he finally realized that her foot-dragging was more than a comic reluctance to trade city for country.

"Not me, darling; it's you I don't want to leave the city. Oh, David, I couldn't bear it if you got stuck in some backwater college! You're too brilliant for that. New York's the art center of this country, not Idaho! I'd do *anything*," she said, "to help you stay here!"

Strange, thought David, that he'd never before noticed how strongly determined the line of her chin could be, how resolute her eyes. He'd always thought of her as a silky blue kitten, and it made him vaguely uneasy to realize she might have a fiercer nature than he'd suspected.

Tendrils of a pungent aroma wreathed themselves around Piers Leyden's nostrils and brought him back to consciousness. Groaning, he sat up on the furry chaise longue. His neck was unbearably stiff, and a dull red pain, beginning at the back of his head, pulsated up through his temples with each small movement he made.

The aroma defined itself: cinnamon. Hot cinnamon buns lavishly smeared with thick sugar frosting, drenched in butter and studded with disgusting raisins and— *merde*—was that the smell of *bacon* mingling with the spice?

His stomach recoiled at the idea of bacon, too. Thick slabs of Canadian bacon browning in the kitchen below. Sizzling in grease. Greasy strips of meat that would be laid on a greasy plate next to a couple of greasy eggs fried sunny-side up and oozing yellow, viscous—

Leyden pushed off from the chaise longue and lurched for Doris Quinn's red-and-gold bathroom.

When he emerged, whitish green, shaken and weak, he found Doris waiting for him with sympathy, tomato juice and the news that Riley's sister was on her way down from upstate.

"So you'll just have to pull yourself together and leave soon, poor sweetie," she crooned, stroking his neck with cool fingers while he forced himself to drink the juice. Her eyes were clear and unbloodshot, her milky-white skin translucent. In fact, Leyden thought resentfully, her whole body radiated as much dewy freshness as a field of goddamned daisies.

He built himself a backrest of ruffled pillows on her bed and gingerly eased himself down.

"It isn't fair," he grumbled. "You drank twice as much of that Scotch as I did. Why aren't you hung over, too?"

Her vitality always amazed him. It was one of life's ironies that she landed in a Manhattan brownstone instead of an Iowa cornfield.

No, cornfield's the wrong image, he decided, watching as she brushed her golden curls into a sunny aureole. She was too decorative and expensive for any farmyard.

He was suddenly reminded of a little rococo church in southern Germany a few years ago. After a glut of Italian Renaissance cathedrals with their ponderous dark marbles and richly somber stained-glass windows, that German church had burst upon his senses like an explosion of light. Clear crystalline windows on three levels had flooded the interior with sunlight, and everything seemed gold and white: a frothy exuberance of gilt-tipped white marble columns; gold-leafed statues, a bright celestial blue ceiling decorated in gaily colored frescoes; and everywhere sunlight glinting and dancing on sparkling white walls and silver gilt trim.

Such rococo frivolity would have been too much like whipped cream and pineapples for a steady intellectual diet; but for dessert or for dalliance . . .

There must have been some hair of the dog in that tomato juice, Leyden thought, reaching out to gather in her gold-and-whiteness; but she eluded him easily. Half giggling, half shocked, she pushed away his hands and continued dressing.

"Sweetie! You know we can't. Not with poor Riley . . ."

"What about last night?" he demanded.

"I was in shock last night. All those people. Besides, we only got pickled."

"That's for sure! You were being the brave little widow, comforting everyone with flagons. No apples, though."

Doris looked blank. She was better acquainted with the spirit of the Song of Solomon than with its actual contents. She shrugged it off. "Anyhow, we didn't—I mean—well, wasn't Oscar here?"

"Yeah, he was the last to leave. He helped me carry you up here. But then it seems like there was some female who—uh-oh!"

"What?" asked Doris, who'd decided that a simple off-white sheath trimmed in Irish lace looked chaste enough for her new status. She glanced at him in the mirror and, alarmed by his expression, turned to face him. "What is it, sweetie?"

"Did I tell you that the police officer investigating Riley's death is a woman?"

Doris's leaf-green eyes widened. "*She* was here—in this room—last night?" Horrified, she reconstructed the room's appearance when she awoke that morning, and then she let out a sigh of relief.

"It's okay, sweetie. You were on my polar-bear lounge, and you had all your clothes on."

"But you didn't," Leyden reminded her dryly, "and she could hardly have taken me for your chambermaid."

He shrugged. "Oh, what the hell? She's bound to hear
about us anyhow."

"Will she think you had anything to do with Riley's
getting poisoned?" A thought struck Doris and she
frowned. "You didn't, did you, Piersie?"

Leyden winced at that pet name. "Don't be stupid.
It's her job to suspect everybody. Anyhow, I'm not the
only one who hated Riley's guts."

"You're the only one who could've taken me away
from him, though," Doris declared dramatically and threw
herself upon him.

Leyden realized that she was suddenly seeing herself in a flattering new light: a woman worth killing for.
Oh, dear Lord!

Now he was the one to push away entangling hands.
"Didn't you say Riley's sister was on her way?"

"And she's such a dreary, dishwatery sort of person,"
Doris sighed. "Always complaining about her children."
She untwined herself reluctantly. "I guess you'd better
go, sweetie. Uncle Duncan's coming over, too. He's going
to handle all the funeral arrangements. Poor Riley!"

Uncle Duncan was J. Duncan Sylvester, owner and
publisher of *The Loaded Brush*, probably the country's
most widely read and certainly its most influential art
journal. He was a shrewd businessman and a thoroughly
doting bachelor uncle. There were some who said that
Quinn's entrée to the pages of *The Loaded Brush* had
been Sylvester's wedding present to Doris. Her dowry,
said the cattier. At any rate, subsequent acceptance by
that prestigious magazine had been the final entrench-
ment of Riley Quinn's reputation.

And that reminded Leyden: "I told Jake Saxer I'd
pick up the files on the book so he can keep working on
it without disturbing you."

Doris had been examining her exquisite pink nails,
wondering if she should change the enamel to a deeper
red, or if peach would be more appropriate? Now she
looked at Leyden with puzzlement. "But I thought after

that fight he and Riley had that Jake didn't want to have anything more to do with the book."

"Fight? When?"

"Why, night before last. I could hardly hear my television for all the yelling going on down in Riley's study. Jake shouted something about taking Riley to court, and Riley said that if that was the way Jake felt about it, he could go to hell before he got an inch of credit. And then Jake yelled that they'd just see who went to hell first and slammed out of the house. So I thought maybe I'd ask Uncle Duncan if he knows somebody who could finish it."

"Oh, I wouldn't do that," Leyden said silkily. "I'm sure that fight meant nothing. Bringing in somebody new would take longer. Anyhow, Jake's familiar with all the material and knows Riley's style. He'll have the book finished and the royalties in your pocket before you know it."

It took several passionate kisses to distract Doris and remove any lingering hesitations; but when Leyden left the brownstone that morning shortly before eight, he left with the manuscript of Riley Quinn's last book under his arm.

Jake Saxer finished trimming his Vandyke beard and examined the results petulantly. He still wasn't convinced it did as much for his appearance as he'd hoped when he grew it. Maybe because he was too fair-haired? Dark men always looked better in beards for some reason. More saturnine and incisive.

His hand hesitated over a razor, but in the end he decided against removal. After things settled down perhaps, not now. The beard was a disappointment, yet he felt safer behind it. Less chance for an expression to betray him.

He had chosen a carefully casual rust brown suit to wear today, which struck a note midway between Riley Quinn's sartorial elegance and David Wade's graduate sloppiness. After combing his hair, he gave it an artful mussing with his fingers, then nodded in satisfaction. He looked intellectual and reliable but still hip. Of the arts but not too arty.

Only his eyes betrayed a shifting fear and indecision. Had the police heard about his fight with Quinn? Should he bring it up himself? Wouldn't that make it look as if he attached no importance to it, and that it hadn't been a serious thing? On the other hand, if Quinn hadn't mentioned it to anyone, and if Doris Quinn hadn't overheard them, maybe nobody ever had to hear about it. What the police didn't know certainly couldn't hurt him.

Riley Quinn! That double-dyed bastard! After all the work he'd done! The insults he'd swallowed from other faculty members. As if he could be fobbed off with an associate professorship when he'd been *promised*! And damned if Quinn hadn't threatened during their fight to renege on his backing with the college's promotions committee.

Remembered rage held him rigid until he reminded himself that rage was unnecessary now. Riley Quinn was dead. The book would be half his now and carry his name, too, after all; and unless Oscar Nauman suddenly became involved in departmental politics and actively opposed him, his promotion would go on through automatically.

Everything was set. All he had to do now was recast that chapter that had Leyden lumped—rather wittily, too, because say what you will, Riley Quinn had possessed a devastating way with words—with other artists who'd earned Quinn's displeasure or scorn. He could slip Leyden over three chapters and add a couple of paragraphs about him somewhere between Andy Warhol and Chuck Close. That should satisfy Piers Leyden.

14

When Sigrid Harald arrived at headquarters shortly before eight, she found Detective Tildon in her small office with more coffee and the morning papers. The *News* had devoted a full page to Riley Quinn's death, complete with photographs and sensational insinuations about the possible motives behind the poisoning.

The *Times* account was brief, factual and referred its readers to the obituary section where, freed of strict news guidelines, it became gossipy and intimate. In proper order were listed Quinn's degrees, books he'd written and his major pronouncements therein ("Art is not artful for the sake of Art") and the half-dozen artists whose reputations he had personally furthered.

A graceful paragraph commended him for the safe haven he'd provided Janos Karoly after the Hungarian uprising and with unintentional irony went on to say, "Dr. Quinn was the acknowledged authority on Karoly and also the most extensive collector of his works."

In detailing Quinn's career, the article managed, unfortunately, to make his debut in *The Loaded Brush* and his marriage to J. Duncan Sylvester's niece seem as if one were contingent upon the other instead of the happy coincidence Quinn had always insisted on; but it compensated for that by dignifying his running battle with the Friedinger Museum. Quinn's more vituperous remarks had been edited until his attack on that collection sounded objective and Olympian and not at all like the gutter fight it had really been.

Characteristically Detective Tildon had compiled the names of those artists Quinn had—in print and at

scurrilous lengths—sneered at the Friedinger for acquiring; unhappily, none were known to have been near
Vanderlyn College yesterday morning.

Sigrid accepted his list of improbable poisoners
gravely and added it to the pile of data they were amassing on this case. "I don't suppose the lab came up with
any prints on Quinn's cup?"

Tillie's cherubic face was glum. "Just smudges. That
foam doesn't take prints so good. I did notice something
with the lids, though," he said, brightening.

He poked through the box that held most of the
physical evidence gathered at the college the day before,
which the lab had now finished processing, and fished
out two round white plastic lids. Each had an identifying
tag, and Tillie checked with his master list to be certain
he had the correct ones.

Sigrid cradled her own coffee mug in slender fingers
and leaned back in her chair, prepared to be instructed.

"This is the lid from Nauman's cup," the detective
said. "See how the Keppler girl marked it?"

Sigrid duly noted the C/W/SUG on Nauman's cup.

"And this is the one from Quinn's."

Her eyes narrowed as she examined the second lid:
C/W/SUG. Identical except that the W on the lid from the
poisoned cup seemed to be capitalized, while Nauman's
was lowercase. Coincidence or significant difference? A
way of distinguishing the cups?

"What about the other lids?" she asked, searching
through Tillie's voluminous notes. "Didn't one of the
others have coffee with sugar? Here it is: Professor Albert
Simpson. Did you happen to bring along his lid for comparison?"

Tillie was embarrassed. "I didn't think about it," he
confessed. "We just took the contents of the wastebaskets
in the main office."

He looked so stricken over the lapse that Sigrid said
kindly, "Don't worry about it, Tillie. You could hardly
bring in the whole Art Department. If we're over there

later, just check out how she does it ordinarily. See if there's any pattern."

She studied the lids closely and noticed that the letters were slightly smudged on both. The thin plastic was almost mirror smooth. "These should have taken prints readily," she mused.

Tillie nodded. "Good prints of Quinn's right index, middle and ring fingers. Nothing else, even though the kid at the snack bar put the lids on, and Keppler touched them when she wrote across them. Looks like Quinn's was wiped clean before he picked it up."

"Nauman's, too?"

"No prints but his," Tillie confirmed from the lab report.

"Now why would the poisoner take the time to wipe *both* cups?" she wondered aloud.

It seemed logical to Tillie. "Because he touched 'em both. Quinn's when he poured in the poison, and Nauman's when he moved it back."

"Moved it back?"

"That must have been how he got Quinn to take the right cup," Tillie said earnestly. "I've been thinking about how he could have done that."

He brought out the tray Sandy Keppler had used to fetch the beverages and arranged the two lids on it side by side, with Quinn's on the right. "Now, this way there's only a fifty-fifty chance that Quinn'd take the right cup, and our killer wants better odds than that; so he sets Quinn's cup on the right at the very front of the tray, and he puts Nauman's at the very back and on the left.

"I'll bet if you offered any right-handed person— and Quinn was, I checked—a tray set like that, he'd take the front right cup ninety-nine percent of the time. And everybody said Quinn usually got back to the office before Nauman did, so he'd have first choice."

"And if Nauman *had* come back first?" Sigrid asked.

"I guess he'd have found a way to knock the tray

over 'accidentally' and just wait for another time," said Tillie.

"You sound as if you have a particular 'he' in mind."

"Yep. Harley Harris. He was next to the bookcase with plenty of time to doctor the cups while the girl had her back to him. She'd already told him no one could talk to him that morning. So why'd he keep hanging around if it wasn't to make sure Quinn got the right cup?"

"But I thought it was the chairman Harris was angry with, not Quinn. Even though Quinn was the first to tell him he wasn't going to get a degree, Oscar Nauman would seem to be the one with enough authority to keep Harris from getting that M.F.A., and Nauman, after all, was the one who broke their appointment."

Tillie looked confused, but he stuck to his guns. "Well, maybe he'd poisoned the back cup, meaning it for Nauman, and then since he was in Quinn's way, Quinn reached around him and got that one instead of the front cup. And then maybe Harris was so rattled that he let Quinn shut the door in his face before he could knock the cup out of Quinn's hand.

"Sure!" he said, gaining confidence in his revised theory. "And then when Nauman wouldn't give him the time of day, either, that's when he shouted—" here Tillie thumbed through his notebook till he came to a verbatim account of Harley Harris's remarks " '—You just wait then! You'll be sorry! And I hope you roast in hell!' Doesn't that sound like a threat?"

Sigrid was dubious, but before she could voice an alternate opinion, her office door opened, and Lieutenant Duckett stuck his head in.

"Hey, Harald, you handling that Vanderlyn College poisoning? Somebody here to see you about it." Without waiting for her assent, he held the door wide to admit a worried middle-aged man.

Sigrid recognized Duckett's intentional rudeness with an inward sigh, knowing that sooner or later she was going to be forced into a confrontation with him. Duckett was a competent detective and senior to her. He didn't have to feel threatened by her mere presence in the department. If only he could see how pointless these petty little harassments were.

Except for a slight flintiness in her gray eyes, however, Sigrid allowed none of her emotions to show. She rose from behind her battered, regulation desk and invited the man to be seated in the chair Detective Tildon dragged forward.

He hesitated in the doorway, a stocky, forceful businessman of medium height, who was obviously used to taking the bull by the horns and was now momentarily buffaloed at finding the bull was a heifer instead. He quickly regained his composure, but there was still a touch of exasperated impatience as he faced Sigrid.

"Coming to my house. Getting my wife all upset. Wanting to know where's my boy, and I gotta get in touch as soon as he comes home; and then I take him down to the local precinct station, and they say we should come all the way here!

"I'm not saying what he did wasn't wrong, but to send cops! We never had cops before. And then to expect me to come all the way over here, and it's nearly midnight, and nobody but gangsters on the subway that late; so I figure what the hell's so bad about what he's done that can't wait till morning and—"

"You must be Mr. Harris," said Sigrid, interrupting the man's Niagara of words.

"Right. Al Harris. And this is my boy—"

He looked around and realized that he was unaccompanied. With a muttered expletive and a heavenward roll of his eyes he reached around the door frame and hauled in a thin youth whose weak mouth was a pale copy of the older man's more determined one.

"This is my boy, Harley," said Mr. Harris. "He'll tell you all about what he did yesterday."

* * *

"He did what?" growled Oscar Nauman into the mouth-piece of his telephone.

The door to his inner office was open, and in the outer office Lemuel Vance stood by the mail rack sep-arating wheat from chaff, which is to say, sorting his personal mail from Administration's form letters.

Admin. was proud of its ecological efforts in using recycled paper; but here in the Art Department artistic theory held to a cynical belief that recycled paper should be kept recycling. The department's historians were only slightly more conscientious than the artists about reading Admin.'s circulars, so an enormous wastebasket stood next to the mail rack.

"Oh, God! Not the chancellor, too?" roared Nauman.

Vance raised his eyebrows at Sandy Keppler, who had stopped typing and was now frankly eavesdropping. Around the Art Department it was blithely assumed that those who wished to speak privately would close the door.

"Who's on the line?" Vance pantomimed to Sandy.

"Dean of faculties," she mouthed back.

Two girls appeared on the other side of the mail rack. They had entered from the hall door around the corner near Professor Simpson's desk. Sandy knew most of the art majors by sight if not by name, and she didn't recognize this duo in tight jeans, sloppy shirts and tan-gled hair. Moreover, she didn't like the way they gazed around the office so avidly.

"May I help you?" she asked crisply.

"They said Art Department office," drawled one of the girls. "Is this where it happened? Where the guy died?"

Piers Leyden had followed them in, and the com-ment brought a glint of anger to his dark eyes.

"Sorry, my dears," he said caustically, "but the guided tours don't start till next week. Tickets may be pur-chased in the bursar's office. Be sure to tell all your friends."

Cupping an elbow in each strong hand, he quick-marched them back to the hall and shoved them out none too gently. A knot of students clustered near the elevator watched curiously.

"The barbarians are within our gates," murmured Professor Simpson from his book-filled corner as Leyden reentered the office and closed the door.

"It's been like this all morning," Sandy said hotly. "They're ghouls!" She wore a pink-and-blue-checked blouse and well-cut denim slacks that had been prefaded to a soft blue. Her long golden hair was loosely tied back with a matching blue scarf, but her face was pale and distressed this morning. "They keep coming in and staring as if they expect to see someone else dead."

"Chin up, kid," said Leyden, patting her shoulder; but the more pragmatic Vance retrieved two sheets of paper from the wastebasket, and on the blank side he lettered in black charcoal: ART DEPT. BUSINESS ONLY—NO RUBBERNECKERS. Sandy provided thumbtacks, and he fastened a sign on each of the hall doors. Since those doors were always propped open during the day, closing them created an air of siege— an Us-Against-Them feeling.

They had almost forgotten Nauman when from the inner office came another roar.

"Damn his pimpled soul to purple hell! Can't they see he's crazy? Never mind trying to explain. I'll do it myself!"

They heard the phone crash down; drawers banged open and shut while Nauman rummaged for something; then he erupted into the outer office. "Where the hell's a City University directory?" he asked Sandy impatiently.

"Would you like me to get someone on the line for you?" she asked placatingly.

He nodded. "The chancellor."

"Something wrong?" Leyden inquired.

"Those damn copying machines! Invented by fools for the use of cretins!" Nauman's white hair was standing in angry tufts, and he'd bitten the stem of his favorite pipe hard enough to crack it. "If he'd had to copy that letter by hand, he might have come to his senses by the fifth copy. Damn copiers! One for every dean, board member and trustee in the whole bloody city."

He glared at Leyden. "If you *ever* try to sneak another goddamned *primitive* into the graduate program—" he swore.

"I have the chancellor's office on the line," said Sandy.

Nauman glared at Piers Leyden again, then slammed his office door shut. Sandy waited a moment till he'd picked up his phone, then hung up her receiver.

"I take it Harley Harris has surfaced?" asked Leyden.

"I don't know about Harley in the flesh," said Sandy, "but evidently he wrote a letter yesterday accusing the department and especially Professor Nauman of all kinds of improper things, beginning with something like 'the frivolous granting and withholding of graduate degrees.' He must have gone over to the library and run off a couple of dozen, which he hand delivered all over the city. Practically every dean on campus has already called. And as you just heard, even the chancellor and the board of trustees must have got copies."

She looked at Vance disapprovingly. The burly printmaker was choking with silent laughter. "I really don't think Professor Nauman considers it funny, Lem."

"He will!" Vance promised gleefully, and a smile spread over Piers Leyden's face, too, as they topped each other in imagining what the frustrated Harley Harris might have written.

They knew that Nauman felt the department's greatest strength lay in avoiding Administration's notice. As long as Art didn't make annoying demands of the paper pushers and didn't actively embarrass the image polishers, Nauman expected them to leave Art alone and let him get on with the business of imparting knowledge to students as he and his colleagues saw fit.

Quinn's death was bad enough; but Harley Harris's barrage of letters could draw the fire of every nit-picking bureaucrat at Vanderlyn College and could open up an internal investigation that would last longer than any police department's.

15

Sigrid and Tillie had listened to Harley Harris's shame-faced account of his copied letters in astonishment. When he'd finished, Tillie broke the news of Riley Quinn's death, something neither seemed to have been aware of before. Mr. Harris was instantly and indignantly on his guard when he realized that they were interested in his young son not because of his letters full of wild accusations but because they suspected him of murder.

"Okay, so he sent those dumb letters," he told Sigrid. "Dumb! *Dumb! DUMB!*" he reminded Harley, who flinched beneath his father's verbal blows. "But," he said, swinging back to Sigrid, "just because he's dumb doesn't mean he's stupid."

"He uttered a threat in the presence of witnesses," Sigrid said mildly.

"But I didn't mean it!" wailed Harley.

"Shut up!" said his father. "Don't say another word. I'm calling our lawyer."

"If you wish," Sigrid said, pushing the telephone toward him, "but really at this point we're only interested in getting a descriptive statement from your son. The same sort of statement that everyone else who was there yesterday has given us quite freely. Of course, you know best for Harley, and if you feel you want a lawyer present, that's certainly your right."

Again she gestured toward the telephone, and this seemed to mollify the elder Harris. "Tell the lieutenant what she wants to know," he directed the boy.

Point by point Sigrid and Tillie took him through a recital of the previous morning's events.

No, he hadn't touched the cups, and he couldn't tell

you what Nauman or Quinn or any of that bunch drank
while they were wasting time up there. He was always
too busy working down in his studio—"I'm a painter,
not a coffee guzzler"—to hang out with those loud-
mouthed bull tossers. He wouldn't even have been up
there yesterday, except that he'd had an appointment
with Nauman. An appointment *they* had broken, he might
add. Afraid to face him with the real reasons why he
wasn't getting an M.F.A. degree. If his work wasn't any
good, they should have warned him back in December.
Oh, yes, Professor Leyden was his advisor, and yes,
he'd told Harley the rest of the department didn't like
primitives—not that he really was, you understand,
but—

"Keep to the point," growled his father.

Okay. Yeah, he remembered seeing the tray on the
bookcase. Two white foam cups from the cafeteria with
writing on the lids. No, nobody'd touched them while
he was in the office until Quinn came in. "At least, I
don't *think* anybody did," he qualified nervously. His
father snorted derisively. "Okay! *Nobody!*" he cried.

Tillie brought out the tray and handed Harley the
two snap-on lids. "Could you arrange these lids the way
the cups were sitting yesterday morning?"

The boy gnawed his thin lips apprehensively. "They
were just there, side by side. I don't remember anything
special about whether one was in front or anything like
that."

"Christ!" said Mr. Harris. "Call yourself an artist,
and you don't notice details? I can tell you every shoe
in Foot Fair's windows for the last three years."

"I'm not a window designer," whined Harley.

"Oh, yes, you are!" his father said meaningfully.

Pressed hard, Harley admitted remembering that
Quinn had reached behind him to take a cup before
closeting himself in the inner office.

"The one nearest you?" asked Tillie.

"I guess." Quinn had been on his high horse, he
told them; and Nauman was just as rude, acting like he

had nothing to do with getting him canned out of the graduate program.

"Jeez! Two years just down the drain, and what am I going to do now—"

"You'll come into the business with your brother and me as you should've done six years ago," said Mr. Harris.

"But my art—"

"You can paint at night if you want. Or on Sundays. Look at Churchill. Look at Ike. Both of 'em decent painters, but did it stop 'em from winning the war or from running their countries and earning a good living?"

"They were hacks."

"And you're Michelangelo?"

It was evidently an old battle, and Sigrid stepped into it long enough to extract Harley's promise that he'd let them know if he remembered anything else.

When the Harrises, *père et fils*, departed, they were separated by more than a foot of open air; yet Sigrid was left with the distinct impression that Mr. Harris was pulling his son along by the ear.

Tillie rubbed his round chin and admitted that Harley Harris was probably out of it. "That makes it one down and seven to go."

"Seven? Oh, yes, Mike Szabo," Sigrid said dubiously. She had shared with Tillie the background information on Szabo that Nauman had furnished the night before. "He probably had access to the poison closet, but I really don't see how he could have known which of those four cups was for Quinn."

"Still . . ." said Tillie, who hated to leave even the smallest pebble unturned.

Sigrid agreed that it probably wouldn't hurt for him to chase Mike Szabo down and get his statement on the record. "For all we know someone else could have been standing by the bookcase when he brought the tray in and left it."

"If that's the case, I bet I can tell you who it was."

"Who? David Wade?"

Tillie looked deflated that she'd thought of that angle, too, but he pressed on. "That Keppler girl looks like butter wouldn't melt in her mouth, but I bet she'd lie for Wade without blinking those baby-blue eyes."

"When you've finished with Szabo, you might stop by Vanderlyn and ask Keppler where David Wade was yesterday morning; see what her reaction is. And while you're at it," Sigrid added, "better see the dean of—" She had to search through her notes to find the right title. Tillie nodded thoughtfully as she explained what she wanted to know.

For the next couple of hours Sigrid worked steadily at the accumulation of reports on her desk. Gradually the pile dwindled, disappeared; all except for a media query, which she carried to Captain McKinnon.

"Do I have to keep doing these interviews?" she asked sourly, remembering Andrea Ross's gibe about being the Police Department's showcase model.

McKinnon looked at the innocuously worded request. It was from a women's magazine, one slanted toward a readership of women who, if they held jobs, worked more to supplement the family's income than to carve out careers of their own. He tossed it back to her.

"What's wrong, Harald? You ashamed to talk about police work?"

"Of course not! If that's what they'd ask me about," Sigrid said tightly, "but they won't. They'll ask about my personal life—you know, does-my-husband-mind-my-being-a-policewoman sort of thing—and they'll probably think it a waste of time when they find out I haven't got a husband. Anyway, aren't there enough women police officers around that we're not a novelty any longer?"

"Apparently not," McKinnon said heartlessly. "I don't see the problem, Harald. You've conducted enough interviews to know how to steer one."

He held up his hand to forestall further protest. "Look upon it as building up brownie points for the department. Public relations. The commissioner appreciates good public relations."

Sigrid marched back to her small office grimly and telephoned the magazine. Upon being connected with the junior editor who'd requested the interview, she summoned a cordial tone to her voice and expressed her willingness to talk. "Unfortunately my only free time is tomorrow morning at eight A.M."

Silence from the editor, then timidly, "What about lunch, Lieutenant? On us, of course."

"Sorry," Sigrid said. "I have a previous engagement."

"Well, we're not in that big a hurry. What about day *after* tomorrow. We could meet—"

"I'm afraid I'm booked rather solid," Sigrid said firmly. "Perhaps you'd have better luck with someone in a different department. Now Sergeant Louella Dickerson over in Missing Persons . . ."

"Oh, no, Lieutenant. We're all so intrigued with the idea of a woman chasing down murderers, almost a female Kojak. Eight o'clock? I'll certainly be there."

She sounds like a gusher, Sigrid thought pessimistically. She glanced at her watch. Ten-forty and she was due in court at eleven.

It was an appearance connected with a case completed two months before. Routine, but time-consuming. Despite the district attorney's previous promise she wasn't called to testify until after lunch. She wasn't on the stand very long. The defense lawyer had come up against her before, so he didn't try the court's patience by attempting to confuse her in cross-examination. The last time he'd tried that, her cool dignity and unruffled professionalism had convinced a teetering jury of his client's guilt.

She was free a little after two and decided against going back to the office just then. Somehow facing another round of reports seemed unbearably dreary, though she would have denied any touch of spring fever.

Last night's rain had scoured sky, air, and pavements, and in the afternoon sunlight the sky looked bluer

than usual, buildings seemed more sharply edged, and
Central Park's spring foliage shone greener. These things
Sigrid barely noticed as she drove uptown. A short while
later she parked by a fire hydrant almost in front of Riley
Quinn's brownstone and flipped down her sun visor to
reveal a discreet notice that she was on official police
business. As she stepped from her car, what her practical
mind did appreciate about last night's rain was that it
had washed the sidewalks so clean that one didn't have
to watch where one was putting every step—a true boon
considering the city's canine population.

She crossed the street, lightly dodging a chauffeured
limousine. There was a spray of white carnations tied
with black satin ribbons on the gleaming oak door, a
homely old-fashioned symbol that Sigrid hadn't expected
of Riley Quinn's wife.

The woman who answered the doorbell was short
and stout with iron-gray hair, which ballooned improb-
ably around a plain face made even plainer by tear-blotched
skin and swollen red eyes. Hers was the first sign of real
grief for Quinn's death that Sigrid had seen.

The woman seemed to assume that Sigrid had called
to offer condolences. "I'm Millie Minton," she said, taking Sigrid's hand in hers and pressing it sadly as she drew
Sigrid across the threshold, "Riley's sister. It's so good
of you to come."

As tactfully as possible Sigrid retrieved her hand
and identified herself.

"Police!" Mrs. Minton's eyes widened, then flooded
with fresh tears. "Oh, poor Riley! How could anyone
have killed him? It's just so dreadful. What a horrible
way to die!"

"I'm sorry to intrude," Sigrid said uncomfortably,
"but if I might speak to Mrs. Quinn?"

"Yes, of course, Lieutenant." She blew her nose
again with a sodden handkerchief and smoothed her black
dress down over well-corseted hips as she turned.

Beyond the grieving woman the living room was

crowded with earlier callers who had lapsed into discreet conversation. It needed only the tinkle of ice against glass to be mistaken for a well-bred cocktail gathering, though none of last night's bottles and glasses were visible this afternoon. Yet there was soft laughter from one group, which quickly hushed when Mrs. Minton led Sigrid past the open archway. Sigrid found herself scanning the gathering for a tall white-haired figure and was annoyed with herself when she realized what she was doing.

Across the room Jake Saxer flushed and turned away as the full force of her scowl fell on him. Sigrid had been unaware of him until his movement of withdrawal, and her eyes narrowed. Why was he afraid to meet her gaze, she wondered, unconscious of her formidable frown.

Mrs. Minton opened the door to Quinn's study at the end of the wide entrance hall. "I'll tell Doris you're here," she said.

Left alone, Sigrid circled the leather-bound study with interest. Riley Quinn's domain was more or less what she would have expected—pretentiously academic, almost a stage set, yet showing signs of serious work in that rear wall of counters and files. Some still partially open file drawers struck a jarring note in the otherwise precisely ordered room. Had Quinn removed a folder hurriedly on his way to Vanderlyn yesterday morning? And what had he used that crowbar for? Surely it was an odd tool to find standing in the corner of a scholar's study? Visions of monumentally stuck drawers were put aside for the time being, however, as the door opened and Doris Quinn entered.

She was followed by her uncle, courtly and dapper in a gray silk suit and dark red tie. J. Duncan Sylvester was completely bald and had small pointed ears and thick white eyebrows, which he used for emphasis. He looked like an intelligent, wizened elf, and he raised one tufted eyebrow in surprise now. Riley's sister had merely said that a police officer wished to see Doris; she hadn't specified that the lieutenant was female. The publisher of

The Loaded Brush was a thoroughgoing chauvinist where his niece was concerned, and he'd accompanied her to keep some hard-nosed male officer from bullying her. Fleetingly he wondered if he might not be superfluous in this interview.

A second look at Lieutenant Harald's cool gray eyes made him decide he'd better stay after all. Sylvester doted on his niece, but he had no illusions about her mental stature, and this severe-faced young woman looked quite capable of making mincemeat of Doris. He introduced himself, clearly intending to guide the interview.

Sigrid responded politely, but her fullest attention was on Quinn's widow.

If Doris Quinn had shed any tears that morning, no traces of them were visible now. Her leaf green eyes were clear, her skin creamy perfection. She wore an oatmeal-colored dress whose simple cut enhanced her own generous lines and made Sigrid feel stick shaped and ill clothed. She knew, too, that Doris Quinn had sensed her discomfort, for the blonde had visibly relaxed as if she held a secret weapon that made her invulnerable.

Oh, no, you don't, thought Sigrid. She was stung into murmuring coldly, "I'm glad to see you're feeling better this morning, Mrs. Quinn."

Unfazed, Doris smiled sweetly. Long ago she had learned that the best defense is no defense at all—polite apologies and no explanations. "I'm sorry I couldn't speak with you last night, Lieutenant Harald. So inconvenient for you, having to come back twice."

"Not at all," Sigrid said, ashamed of her flash of cattiness now that she had herself back under control.

Unaware of the undercurrents, Sylvester knitted his thick white eyebrows at her. "How close are you to discovering who did this terrible thing, Lieutenant?"

"That's difficult to say, sir. I was hoping Mrs. Quinn might be able to help us."

"Me? How?"

"Were you aware of any conflicts your husband might have been having lately? Did he mention anyone who might have hated him enough to want him dead?"

"No, of course not," said Doris, but her eyes sought her uncle's counsel.

"Marc Humphries was furious about Riley's review last month," Sylvester said after brief concentration, "but I know for a fact that he's been in Japan since last week. What about Karoly's nephew?"

"That funny little Hungarian?" asked Doris. "Riley fussed about him being at the college, but they weren't actually fighting still. Not lately."

Sigrid heard the dubious tone in her voice. "There was someone more recent, wasn't there?"

"We-ell . . . Oh, but I'm *sure* it didn't mean anything."

Sigrid persisted until Doris finally said, "He and Jake Saxer had a fight the night before last." She described what she'd overheard between the two men, and Sigrid had the impression that she was repeating words she'd spoken before—though not to her uncle. Sylvester's keen blue eyes darted attentively back and forth between the two women.

"Arguments are almost inevitable between collaborators," he interposed smoothly, "especially when a book is taking its final shape, and one has to be ruthless about what's included and what must—by the exigencies of space—be omitted. Each tends to play devil's advocate for every example the other wishes to exclude."

Sigrid let that pass undebated. "And you can think of no one else, Mrs. Quinn? Did he ever mention conflicts with students or colleagues?"

Doris Quinn shook her elegant blond head emphatically, but Sigrid still sensed a holding back. Who was she protecting? Leyden? She started to frame another question, but they were interrupted by Millie Minton, who seemed flustered as she opened the door.

"There's a person here who—"

The person in question was stocky and pugnacious, dark of hair and broad of face, and he elbowed past Mrs. Minton, who still stood in the doorway, nodded to her genially and closed the door, leaving her outside. "Mrs. Quinn?" he asked, looking from Sigrid to Doris.

Doris nodded, and the young man strode across the study's Persian rug to hand her an official-looking document.

"What's that?" cried Sylvester.

"A restraining order barring the sale and/or disposal of any artworks of any kind allegedly belonging to the estate of the late Riley Quinn," the stranger said cheerfully. His beautifully cut dark green suit and crisp striped tie contrasted with his cocky street-fighter body, and Sigrid caught a hint of smugness in his tone.

"*Allegedly?*" she queried.

The man had merry black eyes that twinkled when they met her gray ones, as if the two of them shared a very rich joke. Sigrid began to suspect they might, and she moved aside as J. Duncan Sylvester beetled his tufted brows angrily as demanded to know who he was, and what he meant by barging into a house of bereavement like this?

"My name is Stephen Laszlo," said the stocky stranger, handing Sylvester a card.

"An attorney? Whom do you represent?"

"Michael Szabo," smiled the lawyer, "nephew and rightful heir of Janos Karoly."

"Oh, for God's sake! Is he digging that up again?" Sylvester turned to Doris. "Riley must have had a copy of Karoly's will here someplace, honey. See if you can find it for Mr.—" He looked at the lawyer's card distastefully. "Ah, yes, Mr. Laszlo."

"Don't bother," said Laszlo cheerfully. "I've seen it."

"And you doubt its authenticity?" Sylvester's tone was glacial.

"Certainly not!" said Laszlo, feigning shocked anxiety. "You don't, either, do you? I must warn you we can bring witnesses who will vouch that it's in Karoly's handwriting."

It was the proper approach, thought Sigrid appreciatively, watching Sylvester's face change from anger to caution. "If you accept its legality—" he began.

"Accept? My client insists upon it," beamed Laszlo, thoroughly enjoying himself.

"I don't understand, Uncle Duncan," Doris said plaintively. "Riley always said the pictures were his. Aren't they?"

"Of course they are!" Sylvester snapped.

"No, no," said the lawyer. "On that point we must disagree."

Until then all had remained standing. Now Laszlo considerately offered Doris Quinn one of the leather armchairs and seated himself in another, placing his briefcase on the table between them. Sigrid's lips twitched as he offered to bring a chair for her; she shook her head, preferring to lean against a bookcase where she could watch the comedy unfold. J. Duncan Sylvester, his tufted eyebrows beetling furiously, found himself seated behind Riley Quinn's desk.

"You see, Mrs. Quinn," the young lawyer began confidentially, "we have to ask ourselves why Janos Karoly would leave his entire estate to your husband and completely disinherit his own blood nephew?"

"He liked Riley," said Doris. "Riley helped him, and it was Karoly's way of repaying him."

"Now, Doris," said Sylvester, "that was before you met Riley and—"

"But he told me all about it," Doris said indignantly. "Karoly trusted him and wanted him to have the pictures."

" 'Karoly trusted him!' " Stephen Laszlo repeated her words as if they were a gift from heaven. He smiled at Sylvester and Sigrid. "I do hope you'll both remember that if you're called upon to testify." He turned back to Mrs. Quinn. "Of course he trusted your husband. It was a noble thing Dr. Quinn did—helping Karoly come to

America, giving him a place to live and paint. But why did he come to America at all, Mrs. Quinn? Do you know?"

Sylvester drummed his fingers on the leather desk top impatiently. "We've no need of history lessons, Mr. Laszlo. You know as well as anyone else that he came because the Communist takeover in Hungary made it unsafe for him to remain there."

"You're quite right, Mr. Sylvester, I do know." Deliberately Laszlo forced their awareness of the almost imperceptible accent that underlay his own speech. "In 1956 it became unsafe for anyone to mention freedom in Hungary. In speech, in literature and in art. Had he remained, Janos Karoly would have been shot, his paintings burned as decadent trash. It was that way in '56, '57, '58, '59."

The numbers fell like hammer blows, and Sigrid decided he was probably an excellent courtroom lawyer.

"And it was still so in 1960," Laszlo continued inexorably, "the year Janos Karoly, knowing he was an old man who could not outlive the Communist regime, made his will and died."

"A will that left everything to Riley Quinn," Sylvester repeated doggedly.

"Because he trusted Quinn to hold them for his nephew!" Laszlo thundered.

"Rubbish!"

In lieu of further argument Stephen Laszlo opened his briefcase and took out several papers. He gave one to Doris Quinn and two others to the bald publisher. "I have extras," he told Sigrid, his black eyes dancing again. "Would you care to see one, Miss—"

"Lieutenant," corrected Doris, automatically remembering the duties of a hostess. "This is Lieutenant Harald from the Police Department."

"Uh-oh!" said the lawyer. Then he shrugged and gave Sigrid a copy anyhow.

"Uh-oh, indeed!" said Sylvester grimly. "Where did you get this?"

"What is it?" cried Doris. "I can't read it."

"Here's a rough translation, Mrs. Quinn," he said helpfully, handing her a copy of the second paper he'd given her uncle.

Sigrid quickly scanned her two sheets. The first was a photocopy of a page from an artist's notebook, about fourteen inches square. There were small pen-and-ink sketches on the page, some partially obliterated by a spiky European handwriting. The first half of the page, dated *3 août 1960*, was in French and seemed related to problems illustrated by the sketches. The bottom lapsed into a language she didn't understand but suspected was Hungarian.

On the second sheet was a translation of the entire page. She skimmed through the part about the drawings— something about a "nexus"—which seemed to have continued into Hungarian as it became more technical about color theory and the mathematics of wave patterns. Abruptly the subject changed from the abstract to the personal:

> . . . *today have I written my will, trusting all to R. The hellhounds who ravage my homeland will have nothing of me. When I am dead, my pictures will begin to be worth much. R. has promised to help my nephew escape and come also to this country. When he comes, my paintings will be a rich inheritance for this child of my sister. Blood of my father's blood. It pains me that I cannot write this in my will, but R. says that to do so would be to endanger my nephew's chances of ever escaping. That the government here would have to send my pictures there because he is still a citizen of Hungary. O my country! How thy son grieves for thy interconnected hills, nexus of my life . . . !*

The writing returned to technical problems of light and color.

"Doris," said Sylvester in an odd voice, "where did Riley keep Karoly's notebooks?"

The blond widow looked blank. "Notebooks?"

"Did he have a safe?"

Doris shook her head. "Would they be on the bookcase?"

"Try the file cabinets," Sigrid suggested, pointing to a drawer that was still slightly open, "but I'd use a pencil if I were you. There might be fingerprints."

The drawer included the *K* section of the alphabet, and it was obvious that at least two inches of material were missing.

"By thunder, you're a witness, Lieutenant!" Sylvester cried. "Arrest that man! He and Szabo have stolen the notebooks."

Doris Quinn chose that moment to discover the crowbar. "What's this thing doing here?"

"Put that down!" her uncle ordered crossly. "It probably has fingerprints, too."

"I doubt it," said Laszlo. "Anybody who's ever watched a week of American television knows enough to wear gloves."

"There, you see? He admits it," said Sylvester. "They arrive like vultures the minute Riley is dead, use a crowbar to break in, ransack the files, steal the notebooks—"

"Was the door forced?" Sigrid asked. "I didn't notice."

"It was unlocked when P—" Doris caught herself. "When I opened it this morning," she amended.

"It seems to me you aren't taking this very seriously," Sylvester told Sigrid.

"If you think there's sufficient evidence for arrest," Sigrid answered, "then you should call your local precinct station. This isn't my jurisdiction, and I'm not in Burglary."

"But there's the crowbar." He noticed a metallic labeling tape on the tool and bent his round bald head closer: " 'Property of Vanderlyn College, CUNY.' That proves it."

"What does it prove?" asked Laszlo. "Dr. Quinn could have borrowed it himself."

"Well, he sure as hell didn't lend Szabo those notebooks! How do you explain that?"

"I don't," shrugged the lawyer. "How they entered my client's possession is not my concern, and unless you can prove culpability," he added sternly, "I should remind you of the laws of slander. Anyhow, my client no longer has them. They've been turned over to the custody of the courts, and there they'll remain until legal ownership of Janos Karoly's estate is settled."

He nodded to Sigrid, bowed to Doris. "Good day, Lieutenant, Mrs. Quinn. I'll see myself out, thanks."

"What does he mean, Uncle Duncan?" asked Doris when the lawyer had gone. "Karoly's estate *was* settled. Riley even sold some of the pictures to pay the inheritance taxes."

Sylvester seemed not to have heard her. He was staring at the photocopies Laszlo had given him. "Poor Riley," he said at last. "I used to wonder why he didn't publish the notebooks. In spite of everything he was a true historian. He must have known Karoly mixed in damaging personal remarks when he wrote in Hungarian, but *New World Nexus* was Karoly's greatest painting, and he couldn't bring himself to destroy any of the artist's notes on the creation of such a masterpiece."

He picked up the restraining order Stephen Laszlo had brought and looked over at his niece. "We shall have to get you a very good lawyer, my dear."

16

Sigrid glanced up at the sound of a tap on her half-opened door and smiled a welcome as Tillie poked his head in to see if she were free. Those unconsciously given smiles of genuine liking were so rare that one forgot between times how gravely sweet they were. Not for the first time Tillie paused, wishing Duckett or Lyles could see her smile like that. Maybe then they'd understand why he liked working with her, and why he was one of the few men in the bureau who didn't consider Lieutenant Harald a sexless automaton.

"Any success?" she asked.

He nodded and reported on several unrelated matters that had filled his day before getting around to the Vanderlyn College death. "I finally caught up with Mike Szabo at his boardinghouse this afternoon. He seemed a little nervous when I first identified myself. Said he wouldn't talk without his lawyer."

"I just met that lawyer, and he's sharper than a stiletto."

"Yeah? Oh, well, it didn't matter because as soon as I asked him about yesterday morning, he loosened up. Didn't seem to bother him a bit to answer all my questions."

"He was probably too relieved to realize that you weren't interested in his whereabouts last night," Sigrid said and then told him about the Vanderlyn College crowbar, the stolen notebooks and the restraining order Stephen Laszlo had served on Doris Quinn.

"So Quinn *did* rook him out of his inheritance," Tillie exclaimed. "That's why Szabo was acting like the cat that swallowed a bowl of canaries. When his landlady asked him if today was a holiday, he told her that every day was from now on. That he was going to be rich. He wouldn't say how, but he answered everything else I asked him. He swears no one was in the outer office when he carried in the tray and set it on the bookcase. Unless he's a better actor than I'd give him credit for, I don't think it even crossed his mind that we'd accuse him of putting poison in Quinn's cup. He says he was never in the printing studio and didn't know it had a storage closet.

"I stopped in at Buildings and Grounds over at the college. There aren't any master keys for those special locks, and the girl on the desk says that someone like Mike Szabo—maintenance personnel—just wouldn't have access to the duplicates."

"So we're left with two down and six to go?" asked Sigrid. "Or is it seven?" She sensed a suppressed satisfaction behind the detective's cherubic face and was willing to let him work his way around to its source in his own methodical way.

"Just six. I met David Wade in the cafeteria and casually asked him if he'd been up in the Art Department yesterday during all the excitement."

"And?"

"At the library all morning. I checked. He was in the reserve stacks. No mistake. There's only one entrance into that area, and it's gimmicked with some sort of magnetic alarm that goes off if anyone tries to sneak a book out. There's a desk where you have to sign in and out, and the librarian showed me the time sheets: in at nine-forty; out at twelve-fifteen."

"What about the dean of faculties?"

Now they'd come to it.

"Your hunch was right." Tillie beamed. "Nauman's meeting with the dean wasn't about anything crucial, and his secretary says she made that clear when she called at such short notice yesterday morning. She seemed surprised to hear that Nauman had a previously scheduled appointment for that same time and wondered why the Keppler girl didn't suggest another date for Nauman to see the dean."

He looked at Sigrid expectantly, but she wasn't quite prepared to share his surmises. Her curiosity about the odd lapse in the competent young secretary's efficiency had been a shot in the dark, and after all, what did it prove? She tipped her chair back until it rested on its two rear legs and wedged her knee onto the edge of her desk.

"What did Keppler accomplish by double scheduling Nauman?" she mused aloud.

"It wouldn't have kept him from being there when Quinn drank his coffee," said Tillie. "Classes were over at ten-fifty; his appointment with the dean was at eleven-fifteen. Anyhow, he still could have seen Harris at eleven if he'd wanted to. The dean's office is just three floors down."

Sigrid thought about that and agreed. "Fifteen minutes should have been long enough to make it clear he wasn't going to reverse the committee's decision. The only thing canceling Harley Harris accomplished was to make him angry all over again."

Tillie resorted to his notes again, leafing through them as if they held the answer concealed in his neat script. At times like this he was humbly aware of his lack of imagination. The book made no mention of intuition, but he knew two and two didn't always make four even when it looked as though they should.

"I guess I'm being rather stupid about this case," Sigrid said, letting her chair hit the floor on all four legs. "After all, life's not a convoluted double-crostic. Why shouldn't the simplest explanation be the right one?"

"She had plenty of opportunity," Tillie encouraged. He cited chapter and verse, but Sigrid waved it aside impatiently.

"We could build an airtight case against Sandy Keppler if all we needed was opportunity. Give me a motive, Tillie! Why would she do it? There's no logical reason.

Nauman says that as soon as she and Wade are married, they'll probably leave New York. No, we need someone with a more solid motive. Someone like Jake Saxer. He and Quinn had a loud fight the night before last. Sounds very much as if Quinn were kicking him off their book project." She repeated Doris Quinn's account, and Tillie perked up.

"What if he had the door cracked when Szabo brought in the tray? Then when Keppler took the hot chocolate in to Vance—" He brought out his sketch of the Art Department floor plan and pointed to the partition separating Vance's office from Nauman's. "I don't know how thick that wall is, but he might have been able to hear them talking. From the inner office to the bookcase and back is only thirty seconds, and that includes doctoring the coffee and putting the lid back on and wiping it. I timed it. Forty-five seconds for the others."

He was looking at his watch as he spoke, watching the sweep of the second hand. Suddenly he focused on the time itself and bounded to his feet. "I promised Chuck I'd leave on time today," he exclaimed, his round face guilt-stricken. "He's trying out for shortstop in Little League, and I'm supposed to help him with his fielding."

Sigrid inclined her head and paraphrased an old Henry Morgan weather report. "April showers followed by small boys with baseball bats?"

"You'd better believe it! And out-of-shape dads with sore pitching arms." Tillie grinned as he rushed from the room.

A short while later Sigrid stood in the parking lot feeling suddenly edgy and restless. She unlocked her car, drove to the exit and paused indecisively. The sun was still high; it was too early for dinner, and besides, that odd sensation wasn't hunger even though she couldn't put a true name to it. Spring fever? Absurd! She gave herself a mental shake and drove over to her favorite health spa. Twenty laps of the pool left her pleasantly tired and in a better mood. On the way home she stopped in at a grocery close to her apartment and brought a frozen chicken potpie for dinner later.

When she got home, she changed into jeans and an old shirt and went down the hall to a cubbyhole formally referred to as "bedroom #2" on the rental agent's diagram, but which in Sigrid's case had devolved into a storage closet/workroom. The rest of the apartment was almost Spartan in its bare neatness; this room held the small amount of messiness Sigrid allowed in her life. Its latest addition both fascinated and appalled her.

Once a week large open trucks from the Sanitation Department make the rounds through Manhattan. On the night before, citizens wanting to rid themselves of old mattresses, dilapidated sofas, defunct refrigerators or any such furnishings too large for the regular garbage trucks, may stack these items on the sidewalk for early-morning pickup. Other citizens spend that same evening picking through the leavings. One person's trash truly becomes another's treasure, and scavenging is considered a respectable pastime.

Sigrid had never indulged in the sport. Her furniture came from a proper store and was all modern, with neutral-colored no-nonsense fabrics and clean, functional lines. When her cousins cooed over Grandmother Lattimore's Chippendale piecrust tables or her Queen Anne highboy, delicately asserting nebulous claims in case grandmother wished to dispose of anything, Sigrid had always yawned and gone off with a book. Yet two weeks ago, walking home from the Laundromat, she had paused by a motley collection of castoffs near the curb.

Standing slightly apart, as if to separate itself from the rest of the debris, was a perfectly horrible armchair. It was square and massive, and the wood was slathered in thick layers of brown enamel, like peeling alligator skin. The seat and a central back panel were upholstered in cracked brown leather. The wooden back itself rose to a height of five feet, and instead of knobs its two uprights ended in roughly carved lions' heads. Another pair of snarling long-toothed lions' heads appeared on the ends of the broad armrests. All four were as large as a domestic cat's head. Except for simple bevelings and turnings the rest of the wood was unornamented.

Sigrid had stopped short at the sight of it, held by an inexplicable attraction. She was not the sort to talk about character in a piece of furniture, yet something about that hideous chair . . .

She'd hesitated, measuring its mass against her strength. Ridiculous. She'd shrugged and walked on. At the far end of the block she saw a young man and woman dressed in identical Levi's and shirts. She saw the man point to the collection of things behind her, saw the woman's interest revealed by a quickened pace. In that instant Sigrid knew they would want the chair and just as instantly knew that she was closer. Without stopping to analyze her decision, she turned back, slung her laundry bag into the chair and began tugging it down the sidewalk. She saw the envious glance the young couple gave her as they passed and felt a small pride of ownership mixed with a large portion of embarrassment. An adolescent from her building overtook her and offered to help drag her booty home; fortunately the elevator was empty so they were able to get it upstairs and into her apartment without enduring curious stares.

The next day a helpful clerk at a nearby hardware store sold Sigrid paint remover, sandpaper and steel wool and gave her enough enthusiastic (and free) advice to make her succumb to the refinishing bug. The mindless activity was perfect for unwinding, yet physical enough to compensate for those days when she'd had to shuffle papers for eight hours. As she scraped and sanded and stripped away the old paint, she was even more delighted by the chair. Especially when judicious applications of the paint remover revealed that the lions' eyes were inset with clear green glass marbles.

She had no idea what wood the chair was made of, knowing only that it was close-grained and had a mellow tone. Beneath the brittle brown leather she'd found horse-

hair and cotton padding, which the hardware-store clerk
advised her to try to salvage since it was probably the
original. In her mind's eye she pictured the chair waxed
to a soft gleam. She hadn't quite decided on new fabric,
but moss-green velvet kept floating into that mental picture.

What she would do with the damn thing when she
finished it, she hadn't the least idea. Nor did she want
to look that far ahead. For the time being, all she cared
about was the pleasure she derived from freeing the wood
of its coat of ugly brown paint.

But somehow she couldn't settle into it this evening.
Her earlier restlessness had returned. At last she threw
down the sandpaper and went into her bedroom to sit
cross-legged in the middle of her bed, an elbow on each
leg, her chin supported by her cupped hands. From early
childhood this had been her soul-searching position, and
she still reverted to it when troubled.

So what was the matter? Was it a residue from last
night? Was she in fact jealous of Cousin Hilda after all?
Examined psyche answered *no*. Then did she regret not
having a Chuck to keep promises to as did Detective
Tildon? It was a relief to face this squarely; an even
greater relief after honest examination to know she was
not getting broody about children.

So what was left? Work, of course. Duckett's continued antagonism and that blasted interview first thing
in the morning. Better make a special effort in clothes
tomorrow in case that editor brought along a camera. As
for her case loads, all were well in hand except for Riley
Quinn's death.

If only there were some way to ascertain how the
killer had known for sure which cup the deputy chairman
would take. That was the key. Unless Keppler did it, in
which case knowledge was a simple matter of a capital
W on the lid. But if it were Keppler, what was her reason
for wanting Quinn dead? Any of the others, even Vance
with his resentment of art historians or Simpson with his
promotion, had more motive than the pretty young sec-

retary. And there was Mike Szabo scheming for Karoly's paintings and Harris's anger about his failure.

Opportunity without plausible motive; motives without provable opportunity. Round and round it went, and yet she couldn't help feeling that somewhere in the past two days something she'd heard or seen or been told held the answer. She started with Harley Harris and worked her way up to Professor Simpson and then back down to Harris again without spotting it.

If Harris could be believed, there was nothing unusual about the positioning of the cups; but the poison had been in Quinn's cup and not in Nauman's. Fantastic suppositions danced through her mind: could Riley Quinn have been a secret sugar addict? Could he have kept extra packets of sugar in his desk drawer to add to his already sweetened coffee, and could the poisoner have doctored the packets, substituting potassium dichromate? But the chemical was orange, dammit! Quinn would have noticed orange sugar. Unless he were color-blind?

Oh, God, a color-blind art critic! And she was the one who'd preached simplicity to Tillie.

All right, then, what's simplest?

That the killer had been a regular at the morning coffee breaks.

Agreed.

That he had noticed whether Quinn habitually went for the left or right cup.

Agreed.

That he (not forgetting that "he" could be Ross or Keppler) had been in the office when Quinn picked up the cup so that he could—à la Tillie's first theory—knock over the tray before Nauman arrived if Quinn picked the wrong cup. (And it might be worthwhile to ask if the tray *had* been upset in the recent past.)

So!

She concentrated on those three points. If logic served, Harley Harris and Mike Szabo were again eliminated on the first two points alone, and even without the librarian's alibi David Wade was eliminated by the third point. As was Professor Simpson? By all accounts he hadn't entered the room until after Quinn had gone through to the inner office. So who did that leave in position to see precisely which cup Quinn took?

She tried to visualize Sandy Keppler's large office, collating all their statements. When Quinn chose the fatal cup, Sandy had been at her desk, Andrea Ross and Piers Leyden had stood talking by the mail rack, Vance had been waiting by the file cabinets to corner Nauman for a discussion of printing presses, and Saxer— Irritably she tried to place Jake Saxer in the room and failed.

Another point to check on.

Keppler, Ross, Leyden, Vance, and Saxer. Could any of these be eliminated? Tentatively she removed Lemuel Vance's name. He seemed to have a hot temper, so wouldn't poison be too calculated? Especially since his strongest grudge against Quinn seemed to be an annual irritation about budget priorities or the usual friction between artist and art critic.

And still no feasible motive for Sandy Keppler. Revenge was a strong motive for Ross, plus getting her promotion after all, since Quinn's death opened up another professorship. Saxer kept his stakes in Quinn's book, and Piers Leyden kept his professional reputation safe from Quinn's vitriolic criticism. She and Tillie would have to hammer at those four until one of them cracked, or someone remembered a previously overlooked point. Which one, though?

When the telephone rang, she was so tired of the squirrel cage her mind had become that she welcomed its interruption.

"Miss Harald? This is Roman Tramegra. I *do* hope I'm not disturbing you?"

Sigrid reassured him.

"I tried to call you earlier—last-minute invitations are so gauche, don't you think—but you weren't in, so I'll just have to be gauche *any*how."

"Not at all," Sigrid murmured, a trifle bewildered. Tramegra's deep bass voice was so at variance with the

frivolous nature of his remarks that she had trouble rec-
onciling the two.

"I've felt *such* a Nosy Parker all day, moving your
mother's things out of the way, and I *still* can't find
everything. I say, do you suppose I could bribe you into
coming over if I told you I have a wonderful lasagna in
the oven? It's real mozzarella. I smuggled a ball in from
Italy last night—you mustn't report me—the customs
inspector thought it was some sort of soap on a rope for
the shower. They're *quite* thick. *Do* say you'll come."

Sigrid weighed the invitation and decided that Mr.
Tramegra was exactly what she needed to take her mind
off work. "It's kind of you to ask me. Lasagna sounds a
lot better than the frozen potpie I was going to thaw."

"Now don't bother to change," he boomed. "Just
come as you are. I'm not dressing, and the lasagna'll be
out of the oven in twenty-five minutes."

Sigrid promised she would be there in time. She
brushed out her long dark hair and, instead of rebraiding
it, let it hang loose down her back, secured only by a
white scarf. She kept the jeans but exchanged a fresh
blue and white shirt for the frayed chambray, which had
paint-remover stains down its front. In less than five
minutes after Tramegra's call she had gathered up her
black shoulder bag and the *Life* article that she'd borrowed from Anne's files and was on her way.

17

"**W**ho can find a punctual woman? Her price is above rubies!" chanted Tramegra in his basso profundo as he opened the door to Sigrid's ring.

Last night the Great White Hunter, tonight a fugitive from a yacht club, Tramegra wore rope-soled sneakers, white duck slacks and a navy-and-white polka-dot scarf tucked into the open neck of his navy shirt. An aroma of burned tomato sauce wafted through her mother's apartment.

"Just the tiniest bit charred around the edges. Won't hurt it a bit. In fact, it adds a certain piquancy to the flavor," he assured Sigrid, whisking her into the dining area.

Somewhere he'd found a red-checked tablecloth and a wrought-iron candelabrum that Anne had picked up in Spain. By candlelight the place looked homey, cheerful, and above all neat.

"It hasn't looked this good since the day Mother moved in," Sigrid told him, diverted by the novelty of walking through the apartment without stumbling over something.

Tramegra accepted her praise but admitted, "I took shortcuts. And whenever I was *completely* baffled by where to put something, I stuck it in Anne's bedroom. Perhaps after dinner you could look through the things in there and help?"

He brought in the casserole, and he'd been right. The slight charring hadn't hurt the flavor at all. Sigrid was hungry by then and ate the lasagna with enjoyment. Also the garlic bread. The Chianti was cheap but drinkable. The salad, however . . .

"You don't like the salad?" asked Tramegra.

"I expect it's the anise," Sigrid answered as diplomatically as possible.

"Now you know, I truly hesitated over whether or not to add anise. Not everyone cares for it, but it's so typically Italian. Oh, not with an oil-and-vinegar dressing perhaps, but plain oil and vinegar are *so* unadventurous, and cooking should always be an adventure, don't you agree?"

Without waiting for an answer, he described a cooking contest he'd won a few years back with a stuffed-artichoke dish of his own invention. "Well, not *won* actually, but second place is nothing to be ashamed of. Especially when the prize is five hundred dollars. *That* kept the wolf from my door a tidy few weeks. And then I wrote up my experiences as a cooking contest entrant, which I sold to three separate magazines." He named them, but Sigrid didn't recognize any of the titles.

As dinner progressed, she found herself warming to the man. He still reminded her of Grandmother Lattimore's pampered Persian, but there was more to him than that. His eyelids were heavily hooded—what Sigrid thought of as Elizabethan; but beneath those hoods his eyes were alert and knowing. There was an absurd pomposity about him that never quite slipped over into buffoonery, until one could almost suspect him of having constructed an elaborate protective facade. He chattered on about himself in that deep voice, as unselfconscious as a child. A bright, self-centered child who looked at the world through unjaundiced, inquisitive eyes.

By meal's end they were on a first-name basis, and Tramegra waved off her help in clearing the table. "I'll just whisk these into the dishwasher and start the coffee, and you must see what you can do with that midden pile."

It was an apposite adjective, Sigrid thought, looking at the muddle on the floor of her mother's room and layering her bed. There were newspaper clippings, a half-eaten box of chocolate liquors (which Sigrid had always considered a dreadful thing to do to either chocolate or liquor), an envelope that held a handful of turquoise beads and a broken silver chain, several pair of panty hose, an extra venetian blind, shoes, letters without envelopes, odd bits of photographic gear and most of the clothing Anne hadn't taken to Italy with her this time.

Anne Harald was not unhygienic, but the litter she could strew was phenomenal. She was the type who pulled furniture into the middle of the room in order to vacuum the corners, then forgot to push things back. Or she would take down curtains to clean the windows and leave them piled on a chair for a week.

Tramegra had tactfully left a large wastebasket just inside the door, and Sigrid came close to filling it, knowing that if her mother had valued any of the papers, she would have filed them promptly. Sigrid was just clipping the last skirt onto a hanger in Anne's closet when Tramegra paused in the open doorway.

"Excellent, my dear! Simply excellent. Come along now. You've *earned* your dessert."

Even though he was still comparatively young, he had fallen into an avuncular manner with her, which eased her usual stiffness. She didn't feel she was being "drawn out" because Tramegra seemed perfectly content to do the talking for both of them if necessary.

"I didn't take time to bake today, but there's an adequate bakery in the next block, and these petits fours seemed passable. I made them give me a sample before I'd buy. You should always insist on a taste," he said, pouring coffee from a silver pot into china cups, both of which Sigrid had forgotten Anne even owned, so seldom did her mother use anything except a percolator and mugs imprinted with black and red P & W Railroad logos.

"If a bakery's proud of its product and cares for your patronage, they're always willing to give you a sample.

I did a filler once on how to pick bakeries and delicatessens. I shall have to give you a copy of it."

It was becoming clearer that Roman Tramegra was a journalistic magpie who scraped together a living of sorts on the fringes of authorship and publishing, carefully gathering up a bauble here, a gewgaw there, which he polished into small salable tidbits: household hints, buying tips, brief how-to articles, explications of humorous bits of nonessential information and a multiplicity of filler items for magazines. Most of his markets were small magazines or trade journals, which paid just enough to keep him going; occasionally an article would score with the higher-paying "slicks," and then everything was jam tarts and honey.

"I once wrote two thousand words on how to call a cat in twenty different languages," he said in his dignified rumble, his hooded eyes drolly solemn as he elaborated. "You know—Here, kitty-kitty, in Japanese, Swedish, Choctaw and so forth. *Holiday* bought it first for a most generous sum, then *Cat-Talk* took a second version, and finally *Reader's Digest*. My dear child, it paid the rent for two years!"

He reworked legends on flag lore and major holiday customs, and explained why chimney sweeps wear top hats, or why the fifth borough of New York is called *the* Bronx instead of Bronx. A hundred different subjects.

"How do you think of so many?" asked Sigrid with an amused smile.

"If something catches my eye, makes me stop for a second thought, I jot it down *immediately*. Whenever I see someone doing something unfamiliar, I ask a *million* questions. Mostly, yes, mostly people are flattered that someone's interested. And *really* if a man likes his job, there's simply *no* way he can be boring when he talks about it. Think of the librarian for a symphony orchestra: finding a complete set of scores for all his orchestra members. I mean, you just don't run off a photocopy of the violinist's score and hand it to the oboe player. And the commissary manager of a large zoo: where does he buy mice for the snakes and owls, and live grasshoppers for birds that turn up their fussy little beaks at dead ones?

"Or the curator of an art museum. How does he go about authenticating a dubious painting? Incidentally did you know that Picasso was quite unreliable about that? His early works are often forged, but I've heard there've been cases where he capriciously disavowed things he had actually and truly created. Don't think *that* won't give a museum director white hair!

"Oh, no, my dear, the problem has *never* been thinking up subjects, but selecting. *There's* the difficulty. Everything is grist for my mills. I grind fast," he said with sonorous resonance, "but exceedingly short, unfortunately."

The mangled metaphor made Sigrid laugh, and Tramegra looked pleased. "What a lovely laugh you have, my dear," he said; and before she could become self-conscious about it, he was off on another round of anecdotes.

Sigrid pushed her cup across the newly polished coffee table for a refill and sat listening with one denim leg drawn up, her strong chin supported on her knee.

Tramegra refilled both cups, then padded from the room to get a magazine article he'd written the month before that he thought would interest her. He even walked like a cat, Sigrid thought idly, watching him go. He moved lightly for one his size, each footstep placed precisely and neatly, one in front of the other.

When he returned, he had circled back to a previous point. "Speaking of Picasso forgers, did you know there are artists who forge their own work?" He dumped the contents of a large manila envelope on the couch beside him. "I've been gathering material about it."

"That sounds like a contradiction in terms," said Sigrid. "I know artists often paint several versions of the same subject, but that's not forgery, is it?"

"Not if they're all connected, no. But suppose an

artist in the first flush of youth is entranced with painting blue cubes. For four years, let us say, he does *nothing* but blue cubes—singly, in tiers, or jumbled on top of each other. Then he gets bored; moves on to mauve and puce gardenias. Now further suppose, if you will, that the public has liked his blue cubes but *loathes* these mauve and puce gardenias. Beastly colors, and anyhow, the critics don't think his draftsmanship's as good with flowers as it had been with cubes. Nevertheless, our artist stubbornly perseveres and for twenty years paints gardenias, tiger lilies and tulips, all in mauve and puce. Sooner or later he has to realize that they simply aren't bringing in much capital. In the meantime, seeing that there will be no more pictures of blue cubes, the price has simply skyrocketed. Our artist, starving in his miserable garret, begins to think how jolly it would be if he still had a few of those old canvases around. So one fine day he sneaks around to the local paint store, buys a couple of tubes of ultramarine, and a few weeks later after the paint's had time to dry, he announces to the world the discovery of several forgotten canvases from his blue-cube period. There he is, you see—a forger of his own work."

"But it's still the same artist doing the same sort of picture," Sigrid protested.

"*You* know that and *I* know that and so does the artist," Tramegra agreed cheerfully, "but critics cry foul every time. They say it's not the same, and anyhow—"

He had taken a swallow from the coffee cup and now broke off to stare at it distastefully. Then his brow cleared. "How *silly* of me! I've taken your cup by mistake. How on *earth* can you drink it without sugar?"

He brought her another cup and pointedly pushed it over to her side of the coffee table. The swallow had been so bitter that he added another spoonful of sugar to his already sweetened cup. As he stirred the dark liquid and rattled on—he had switched subjects again and was now onto Tibetan tea flavored with rancid yak butter—Sigrid felt a faint flicker of conjecture. A flicker that steadily brightened into radiant certainty.

Gratified by the expression on her thin face, Roman Tramegra expanded on Montezuma's addiction to cocoa. A fascinating subject, he decided. Perhaps he should write an article on it.

18

As Sigrid crossed the squad room the next morning, she was appalled to hear laughter spilling from her small office and to see a large group of men clustered around the open doorway. With a jolt she remembered the interview. Useless to envisage all the outfits she might have chosen from the Carolina side of her closet. Today's navy suit might be a twin of yesterday's gray one—just as shapeless and selected with just as little thought.

She was annoyed at having to waste good time on such a frivolous thing as this interview. How the hell could she phrase words about her "conflicts" as a woman in a traditional male preserve when her mind was running happily on completing a case against Riley Quinn's murderer?

Lower-ranking detectives stepped aside and melted back to their desks upon becoming aware of her presence, and Sigrid's head was high as she took possession of her office.

"I'm glad to see you've been taken care of, Miss Fielden," she said pleasantly, noting the ministrations of her fellow officers.

They had brought the young woman coffee, doughnuts and the morning papers; and now they were offering themselves as substitute subjects to interview.

"*Ms.* Fielden," said the editor a little breathily, "but *do* call me Iris."

From her past experience Sigrid was quite prepared for a glamorous editor; but most of the interviewers she had met had achieved some balance between the feminine and the businesslike. Ms. Fielden, however, kept

her businesslike qualities—whatever they might be—
well concealed.

She had curls, long eyelashes, and many rings on
her pink-tipped fingers; and she so completely filled a
pink ruffled shirt that the distracted Duckett seemed
unable to tear himself away from Sigrid's office. That Ms.
notwithstanding, Iris Fielden looked about as militant a
feminist as the average Las Vegas chorine, and her manner matched her appearance.

And true to Sigrid's foreboding, the lady gushed.
Still, as Captain McKinnon had pointed out the day before, this was not her first interview. Efficiently she removed Duckett and the rest from her office, closed the
door, then faced Fielden's tape recorder calmly. Whenever the questions strayed from the professional to the
personal, she couched her answers in vague generalities
that would apply to almost any working woman and firmly
steered the conversation back to the job itself. In the
end the young editor was so inundated with facts, figures,
and stacks of police-department publicity pamphlets that
she numbly asked, "What was the name of that sergeant
who works in—Burglary, was it?"

"Missing Persons," Sigrid answered guilelessly.
"Sergeant Louella Dickerson. *Mrs.* Dickerson." Without
the slightest twinge of conscience Sigrid offered Dickerson up on a sacrificial platter, even tucking in a candied
apple to enhance the dish: "I've heard that her husband's
extremely proud of her, but that he worries about her
all the time."

It was sufficient. Appreciatively Ms. Iris Fielden
jotted down directions and telephone numbers, then departed, making her way across the squad room to the
accompaniment of even more appreciative whistles.

Even Detective Tildon, entering the office as she
left, looked bemused until he felt Sigrid's sardonic stare.
He flushed, his cherubic face embarrassed. Despite twelve
years on the force Tillie still believed that a happily
married man shouldn't be looking.

"I wonder if Marian would like a blouse like that?" he said, then flushed again.

Sigrid had met Tillie's wife once: a pleasant-faced birdlike redhead whose chest was even flatter than her own. She rather doubted that Marian Tildon would do justice to a pink ruffled blouse and repressively reminded Tillie of the tasks at hand.

Without going into the details about Roman Tramegra and the previous evening, Sigrid outlined her new theory of how Riley Quinn's killer had made certain he and not Nauman would get the poisoned cup.

Tillie nodded enthusiastically when she'd finished. "That sure takes care of the how," he said, "but why?"

Together they sorted through all the statements they'd been given during the past two days and looked for stronger motives. Everything was too nebulous. It meant another morning of digging.

"Just the same, I wonder why Harley Harris didn't say something," Tillie said.

Sigrid reached for the telephone. "Did we ever ask him?"

It was shortly after ten A.M. when they met again to compare notes at the unmarked cruiser parked behind Van Hoeen Hall.

"Why don't we walk down to the river?" asked Tillie, who responded more directly than Sigrid to spring's quickening transformation. "It's another gorgeous day."

Sigrid looked around and for the first time realized that it *was* a gorgeous day. Once again spring seemed to have arrived while her back was turned. She stepped from the car and followed Tillie down a long brick path, which led to the promenade overlooking the East River.

Short-sleeved students lay on the grass in sheltered nooks close to the buildings, rushing the sunbathing season as they studied or flirted or just enjoyed being outdoors without heavy winter clothes. Overhead a few small

puffs of white cloud had drifted into the April blue sky;
forsythia arched golden branches over a nearby water
fountain, and a double row of yellow buttercups marched
primly along each side of the path. Most of the benches
along the path were occupied, but a breeze blowing in
across the water kept the river walk itself almost deserted. The ropes of wisteria twined about the over-
arching trellis let welcome sunshine through now; later
in the summer the walkway would be a dark tunnel
shaded by thick leaves and sweet with the heavy scent
of purple blossoms. As they paced its sunlit length, there
was a medieval feel to the promenade, which reminded
Sigrid of the reconstructed Cloisters up at Fort Tryon
Park.

She leaned against a brick column, one trousered
leg propped upon a low stone bench, listening to Tillie's
report with only half an ear while she stared moodily
across the blue-gray river at the ugly piers lining the
Brooklyn shore.

Riley Quinn was to be buried tomorrow afternoon.
By all accounts he had been a pompous, arrogant man.
An opportunistic thief and so petty as to use his own
work of scholarship for revenge; yet scholar enough to
save a potentially destructive journal because it chron-
icled the creation of Janos Karoly's masterwork. That was
a saving grace; but even if Quinn had died without a
single virtue, the responsibility of discovering his murderer would still be hers.

Think of it as a puzzle in logistics, she reminded
herself. Or a simple algebraic equation, a solving for x.
Try to forget that x equaled a person who might be a
hundred times more ethical, more humane, more likable
than Riley Quinn. Judgment—thank God—was definitely not her responsibility—only the clear identifica-
tion of the unknown x. Hold to that.

Traffic out on the East River was light this morning.
Gulls wheeled and swooped above an open garbage
scow, and in the middle distance a slow-moving police
launch passed an even slower tug. Downriver from

them a helicopter lifted from a pad at the water's edge, shattering the relative quiet and bringing Sigrid back to the present.

Friday classes in the Art Department still weren't back on schedule this morning, though she and Tillie hadn't interrupted the pace. They had poked around classrooms and offices casually, their questions vague and seemingly unspecific; but between them they had spoken to everyone except Sandy Keppler and Oscar Nauman. David Wade wasn't expected till after eleven, but Tillie had tracked down the graduate student who shared a desk in the Nursery with Wade and had taken that puzzled young woman into an empty classroom for a long talk. His indirect questioning had elicited answers that confirmed Sigrid's earlier hypothesis.

"Does it feel right to you now?" asked Tillie, hoping that Sigrid's intuition would agree with what common sense accepted so completely. He had learned that unraveling the problem was what held the tall, calm-eyed lieutenant's interest. The more complex, the better. Wearing a suspect down, hearing the actual confession, amassing evidence for an airtight prosecution—all the details so reassuring to his methodical soul—left her depressed; so he was relieved to see her nod.

"All we need is confirmation from Professor Nauman," she said, squaring her shoulders decisively as they turned away from the river and headed back to Van Hoeen Hall.

Although a couple of inches shorter, Tillie matched her easy strides. His heart lightened as they moved toward familiar routine. This was one of the easy ones after all; another open-and-shut case.

Just that one tricky bit remaining, he reminded himself as they retraced their steps and merged with a throng of brightly clad students surging into Van Hoeen's side entrance.

In Sandy Keppler's cheerfully shabby plant-filled office Lemuel Vance was amusing Piers Leyden, Andrea Ross, and Sandy herself with a description of an administrative assistant's appraisal of Sam Jordan's contribution to the faculty exhibition. The burly printmaker had a mild talent for mimicry, and he minced across the room as if on high-heeled shoes and looked down his nose at the wastebasket, which his supercilious frown transformed into Jordan's polished-steel sculpture.

"Are you trying to tell me," he asked in an outraged falsetto, "that this represents *my* world?"

Instantly he became the supercool Sam Jordan: "Hey, mama, you trying to tell me it don't?"

Their laughter died as Lieutenant Sigrid Harald, accompanied by Detective Tildon, entered the office. Her slate-cool eyes seemed to catalog and dismiss, although her tone was pleasant enough as she asked, "Is Professor Nauman in now?"

"He's on the telephone," Sandy said nervously.

At that moment his door banged open and Nauman appeared, apparently in fine humor. The sight of the tall policewoman brought him up short.

"More questions, Lieutenant?" he asked blandly.

"If you can spare the time, Professor." She had meant to sound professional, but her voice had gone husky, and she felt a warm flush rising to her cheeks. She knew Tillie was staring at her curiously; fortunately Nauman's attention was on the pipe stem he'd finished biting in two.

"Fire away," he told Sigrid, then immediately asked Sandy, "Do we have any adhesive tape?"

Sigrid remained silent as the girl located a small roll in her desk drawer and handed it to him.

"In private, if you don't mind, Professor Nauman." Her voice was cool and under control again. "You needn't leave," she told the teachers who were edging from the office. "I'm sure Detective Tildon has a few more details to discuss with you."

Quite poised now, she preceded Nauman into his office.

Sandy's blue eyes were wide and worried as the door closed, and she twisted a strand of long blond hair anxiously while Detective Tildon spread his notes and diagrams on the corner table and invited Vance, Leyden and Andrea Ross to join him in yet another reconstruction of Wednesday morning's events.

The cleaning crew had been quite efficient in removing all traces of Riley Quinn's sickness and death from the office he had shared with Oscar Nauman. Only a whiff of carbolic lingered, and even that was quickly being dissipated by a mild spring breeze, which drifted through the tall open windows and which seemed to bring with it a vaguely herbal scent. It made Nauman think of formal summer gardens with clipped boxwood hedges and patterned walks.

He stood by the windowsill, awkwardly trying to hold his broken pipe stem with one hand while he taped it with the other. He kept his eyes on the pipe as if by avoiding her eyes he could avoid questions of poison and murderers; but when he groped for the scissors in a jar on his desk, the bowl of the pipe slipped through his fingers.

"Oh, for heaven's sake!" Sigrid snapped irritably, annoyed by what seemed like cavalier treatment of her in his continued attention to mending a pipe. She laid her notebook down and bent to pick up the pipe, and as she straightened, she caught the lost look on his face, and her tone gentled. "You hold it and I'll tape," she said.

Blue eyes met her gray ones, and part of his mind noted dispassionately that the vague scent of lemon balm emanated from her soft dark hair and not from the spring breezes that ruffled the collar of her blouse. She concentrated on winding the tape neatly. Only half a head shorter than he. There was something infinitely touching in the line of her slender neck, in her finely modeled head as she bent to the task.

He felt as if he were standing on a high precipice, removed, and watching the scene through the wrong end of a telescope.

The temporary mend was complete, the tape cut, yet he was still reacting with only the top, detached surface of consciousness. Time seemed stretched out. He drew her to him, and unlike yesterday she came without resistance. Their lips met, then he was holding her tightly, aware of the passion within himself, sensing—he thought—an answering feeling within her.

And nothing happened.

"Dammit! I don't want your pity!" he snarled, releasing her angrily.

"Then don't kiss me like you're drowning, and I'm the last lifeboat on the lake!" she blazed back at him.

They glared at each other until Sigrid dropped her eyes. She took her notebook from his desk and walked slowly over to the window where she stood gazing out for a long moment, her back to the room and to him.

On the brick walks far below, students crossed back and forth, girls and boys in short sleeves and bright colors beneath the blue spring sky. Sometimes in groups, more often in pairs, they lounged around the central fountain, lay on the grass with open books or walked hand in hand from one building to another. And Sigrid Harald, who had never been in love, found herself thinking about the love of a girl for a boy, of a parent for a child, of a man for a woman, or of scholars for their studies. So many kinds of love, and one had grown so overpowering that Riley Quinn had been killed because that love could be more fulfilled with him out of the way.

Sigrid took a deep breath and turned to face the tall man behind her.

"You can't push it away," she said quietly. "He *was* murdered, you know. We can't just ignore it."

The bleak look had returned to Nauman's face. "You know who it is."

It was a statement, not a question, but Sigrid

nodded. "I think so. Proving it will be another matter without a confession. There are a few more facts I need to know. Tell me about tenure. How is it awarded here?"

Nauman answered that question and the ones that followed factually and tried not to let himself see where they were leading.

19

Schedules seemed to be meaningless today, thought Sandy. All morning she had been aware of the police presence in the department—Lieutenant Harald and Detective Tildon asking questions, probing, adding data to the case they were building. Professor Nauman had looked at her oddly once or twice after his short conference with the policewoman but had revealed nothing of their talk.

It was after eleven before she could go downstairs for coffee. Quinn's classes were canceled, of course; but his students, excited by the recent sensational events, had shown up anyhow and now milled about the halls, embellishing every conjecture and rumor that reached their avid ears.

"I've always wondered what it would take to get perfect attendance," Leyden told Nauman sourly.

The elevator was jammed when Sandy returned from the snack bar, and she had to juggle the tray of beverages as she pushed through the hallway. To her surprise she found everyone assembled in the big outer office. Lieutenant Harald had co-opted her desk again.

"One minute please, Miss Keppler," said Detective Tildon and took the tray from her unprotesting hands. He carried it across the room and set it on her desk. Everyone watched curiously as he and Lieutenant Harald seemed to give the cup lids special scrutiny.

"You didn't stop in at my print shop on the way back upstairs, did you, Sandy?" asked Lemuel Vance in an attempt to lighten the suddenly tense atmosphere.

"Knock it off!" David Wade said tightly from the

corner table, and Sandy's eyes widened as she saw him for the first time. He shrugged to show he was just as puzzled as she to find himself summoned to this gathering.

Detective Tildon returned the tray without a word. Yesterday's fear tightened around Sandy's heart, and her hand trembled as she gave tea to Andrea Ross and Albert Simpson, hot chocolate to Lemuel Vance and Piers Leyden, and coffee with sugar to Oscar Nauman and Jake Saxer. She took her own black coffee to an empty chair next to Professor Simpson. Her hands shook so that when she removed the lid the old classicist kindly handed her his immaculate handkerchief to blot up the spill from her blue plaid slacks.

"Shouldn't young Harris also be here?" Simpson asked, refolding his handkerchief.

"Or is Leyden's primitive still hiding in the jungle?" sneered Vance.

Jake Saxer laughed nervously, then smoothed his yellow beard in embarrassment.

"We've spoken to him, and he had nothing of value to add to this inquiry," Sigrid said calmly in her schoolmarm manner. "For the record I'd like to hear your opinions on whether it would have made a difference if Professor Nauman had got the cup with potassium dichromate instead of Professor Quinn."

"It might to Oscar," suggested Leyden. Nauman shrugged; everyone else looked blank.

"I think she means *cui bono*." said Simpson. "Who profits by his death?"

"Correct," said Sigrid. "Well, let's start with what happens now that Quinn's dead. You, Professor Simpson, will become deputy chairman, which means promotion and a larger salary?"

"If the majority of the department approve. I *am* senior historian."

"Do you need the extra money, Professor?"

"I have no family and my wants are few, Lieutenant,

but you may examine my bank records if you feel it necessary."

"A full professor gets a bigger pension," Vance observed from his chair near the bookcase.

"So he does," Simpson agreed equably. "I hadn't thought of that."

"Of course, there are other rewards," said Sigrid, turning to Jake Saxer. "How much is it worth to be listed as coauthor of an authoritative book rather than an insignificant contributor acknowledged briefly in the preface?"

The historian's pale face flushed. "I earned it! I've done ninety percent of the work for that book. He *promised* me coauthorship before we ever began work!"

"Did you get it in writing?" asked Andrea Ross. "Riley Quinn wouldn't have shared authorship of a grocery list."

"Frigid bitch! You're just jealous because he passed you over."

"Surely you could invent a more crushing line, Jake," Professor Ross smiled icily. With her crisp curls and feminine clothes she looked like a porcelain doll; but beneath her artful makeup her face was pale. "You may have done ninety percent, but that's just the donkeywork. Much as I despised Quinn, I have to admit he was a brilliant historian. His ten percent will bring it all together, make the book a success. Maybe you can stick your name on his work, but none of his brilliance will rub off on you. My advice is to enjoy it while it lasts. Just don't try to write another book all by yourself, Jake, or Lieutenant Harald might have to arrest you for indecent mental exposure!"

Saxer sprang to his feet and for a moment actually seemed about to slap her, but Nauman grabbed his wrist with an unexpectedly strong grip and straight-armed him back into his chair with an ease that belied the force he had used.

"Andrea's right, so just sit down and stop being tiresome," he said. "Continue, Lieutenant."

Their eyes locked, then Sigrid referred to her notes again. "Professor Leyden, I understand that Quinn had planned a thorough hatchet job on you. I believe he called your work the 'pap of Polaroid pop.' "

"Riley was incapable of appreciating neo-realism," Leyden said airily, "and he didn't like my friendship with his wife. We were the best of enemies. You know, I'll probably even miss him."

"So what he planned to write didn't bother you?"

"Don't be naive, Lieutenant—of course it did! The gallery-trotting, picture-buying public is smart enough to read but dumb enough to be influenced by self-proclaimed savants; so I'm very lucky that Doris Quinn is going to accidentally burn some of his notes to that particular chapter."

There was a wicked gleam in Leyden's dark eyes, and Nauman shook his head at the artist's audacity. "So now you'll get to dictate your own version, and Doris'll get the pleasure of your company until the book's safely published."

Except for Detective Tildon everyone in the room knew Doris Quinn, and an undercurrent of ribald laughter swirled through the office.

"Just don't burn yourself out," Vance cautioned.

Sigrid looked at Andrea Ross. "With Quinn dead and Professor Simpson promoted, there's another associate professorship available now?"

Andrea Ross carefully tapped her cigarette ash into her empty cup and nodded.

"And you've admitted bitterness at being passed over the first time?"

Again the woman nodded, and Vance said, "Better remember that, Oscar."

Sigrid rounded on him sharply. "You keep acting as if this were all a big joke, Professor Vance. You were in and out of this office all morning, and you were here just before Professor Quinn picked up his cup and took it inside with him."

"And where's my motive?" taunted the stocky print-maker. "I wasn't in his book, I'm not sleeping with his wife, and he didn't cut me out of a promotion!"

"But if the poison had been meant for Professor Nauman?" she asked softly. "It's my understanding that if the chairman's an artist, the deputy must be a historian and vice versa. If Professor Nauman had taken that cup, Riley Quinn would have become chairman. So who's the artist who would get promoted to full professorship and be made deputy chairman?"

"Now just a minute," cried Vance. "No offense, Oscar, but if I'd meant to kill you, you'd be dead now—not Riley. Besides," he said to Sigrid, "I'm no shoo-in. There're at least ten members of this depart-ment who hate my guts, and who would enjoy voting against me."

He said this proudly, and Sigrid noted wryly that he seemed to rate his standing as an artist by the number and caliber of his enemies.

"If the poison was for Oscar, that lets Saxer and me both out," said Leyden thoughtfully.

Professor Simpson cleared his throat. "Also me, I presume?"

"And you, Professor Ross?" asked Sigrid.

"If you think promotion's a strong enough motive for murder, then I'm still in. Either way an associate professor gets promoted to full, and I'm next in line for the associate."

The medievalist leaned back in her chair and lit another of the cigarettes she'd been chain-smoking all morning. Her brittleness had become even more ap-parent as the net tightened.

"We're like the Mad Hatter's tea party, aren't we, Lieutenant? 'Move down! Move down!' Only there's an extra chair left over at this party and I'm not the only one who benefits either way, am I?"

Piers Leyden had been puzzled by David Wade's

presence, and now he beamed appreciatively. "Why, Andrea, how very perceptive of you!" And he, too, turned to stare at the young lecturer.

David returned their stares in bewilderment. "I don't understand. What's it all got to do with me?"

"Nothing!" cried Sandy, crumpling her empty cup in agitated hands. "He wasn't even here. He was in the library."

"That's true," Sigrid said. "We even have a student aide and a librarian from the reserve stacks who'll swear to it. But *you* were here, Miss Keppler."

"*Sandy?*" said Wade incredulously. "You've got to be spaced out. She's the last person in the whole department! Didn't you know? We're getting married this summer. Probably move to Idaho."

"Why?"

"Because my contract's expired and—oh."

He looked like a man who'd been kicked in the groin, and his eyes were sick as he spoke to Andrea Ross. "That's what you meant about an extra chair left over."

"I'm afraid so," said Sigrid. "Your contract expires in June. They couldn't extend it without offering you tenure, and until Wednesday there wasn't a tenured position open. Now there is. After Professors Simpson and Ross are promoted, there'll be an unfilled position left on the history side. Either way Wade would get tenure, wouldn't he, Professor Nauman?"

Nauman nodded stonily. "A chairman teaches only one course. Riley dead or promoted to chairman—either way—someone would have to take up the slack of his other classes. I was going to speak to David this afternoon. Discuss tenure."

"And who has David Wade's career interest most at heart?" asked Sigrid. "Who very loudly read the warnings on that container of potassium dichromate last month? Who could unlock that chemical closet at her leisure or leave the coffee wherever she chose and maneuver things so as to implicate as many people as

possible? Who could mark the coffee lids and position
the cups on the tray, knowing which Quinn would
pick up?"

"No!" cried Sandy. The white foam cup was now
only a formless ball of plastic that slipped from her nerve-
less fingers as the girl shrank into her chair.

"Yes!" said Sigrid inexorably.

There was a stunned silence as Detective Tildon
read the litany of her rights aloud, a silence broken only
by Sandy Keppler's soft, terrified denials.

When they led her away, a scared and angry David
Wade insisted on going with her.

The six people who remained in the large office
stared at each other, incredulous and bewildered by the
sudden finality of it all.

"She said academic positions were so scarce now,"
murmured Professor Simpson. The white-haired classicist seemed distressed and uncertain. "She chided the
Harris boy for not taking the high rate of unemployment
seriously, but even so . . ."

"I hope Washington doesn't hear of her solution,"
said Vance, but the quip was an automatic, mechanical
response, a numb reaction to the grim reality of Sandy's
arrest.

"I don't believe it," said Nauman, who'd been silent.
"Sometimes I *do* get back first. She wouldn't have left
it to chance."

"You said it yourself, Oscar," Piers Leyden reminded him. "Either way—you dead, or Riley—Wade
would still have got tenure. That's the whole point. It
wouldn't make any difference to her as far as making a
place for Wade on the staff goes. And maybe the chan-
ciness of it made her feel that it was out of her hands.
Up to fate. Kismet."

"Anyhow," said Jake Saxer, fingering his pointed
beard and breathing easily again, "poisoning is tradi-
tionally a woman's method."

"Thanks a lot!" snapped Andrea Ross. "You're saying

that if Sandy weren't guilty, I'd be the only logical alternative?" She stubbed her cigarette and stood up. "I'm going to lunch."

Professor Simpson, still upset, began murmuring about finding a lawyer for Sandy; but before anyone could leave, Rudy Turitto, who taught photography and who, to his great regret, had missed Wednesday's dramatics, burst into the office.

"Where's that Lieutenant Harald?" he demanded excitedly.

When they told him, he dived for the phone book, then quickly dialed a number, forestalling their questions.

"Hello? Police?" he said as the call went through. After identifying himself, he said, "Lieutenant Harald's on her way there, I've been told. As soon as she comes in, have her call me—Art Department, Vanderlyn College. It's very important."

"What's happened, Rudy?" asked Nauman.

"It's Harley Harris! He's downstairs holed up in one of the graduate studios. Says he's remembered something about Riley's death. He was here, wasn't he? Right there by the coffee the whole time before Riley came in? But the little bastard won't say what it is. Says he won't tell it to anyone except Lieutenant Harald."

"What could he know?" Vance asked scornfully. "Anyhow, they've arrested Sandy for it. They figure she killed Riley to make space on the staff for David Wade."

"*Sandy?* But that's terrible! Are they sure? Little Sandy?" Professor Turitto looked distressed as the others nodded. "Oh, well," he said, deflated, "in that case, what the Harris kid saw will just pile on more evidence, I guess."

He turned to go. "I've got a class, Oscar. When the lieutenant calls back, would you give her the message?"

Nauman nodded, but his eyes were speculative

as they rested briefly in turn on everyone still in the room.

Uneasily they began to drift away—some to their desks, others to the elevator. Lunch in the cafeteria wasn't gourmet, but it was quick, and no one felt like lingering over food today.

20

In the studio downstairs Harley Harris paced back and forth in an uneasy ellipse. The studio was small and crammed with canvases, easels and odd-sized stretchers. It had been painted white only two years before, but already the walls were covered with anatomical drawings, mathematical formulas for problems in proportion and perspective, political slogans, and a rather rude caricature of one of the red-tape lovers down in the Registrar's Office.

There were crumpled wads of paper on the floor, and along the baseboard stood a line of coffee cans bristling with dried-up brushes and reeking of rancid turpentine. A trashy, unlovely room, but the light was good, and students with no place of their own to work elsewhere could use it on a shared-time basis.

An enormous purple and orange batik covered a whole corner from floor to ceiling; smaller ones fluttered from the high molding; and one of Harris's prouder efforts—a huge snowscape peopled by tiny, beetlelike figures and titled *Hommage à Brueghel*—filled another corner.

"When the hell are they coming?" the boy fumed and flung himself down at a rickety worktable under the tall window. He picked up a ball-point pen and tried to concentrate on exact details of Wednesday morning.

A breeze from the open window stirred the batik hangings, and Harris looked at them nervously, chewing on his weak underlip.

He jumped as the door opened, and Lemuel Vance stuck his head in. "So you *are* here," said Vance. "Rudy

Turitto said you had a hot little tidbit tucked away in your head."

"I'm waiting for Lieutenant Harald," the boy said, holding the papers in front of his thin chest like a shield.

"And you don't want to unburden your soul to anyone else first?" asked Vance hopefully.

"N-no!"

"How tiresome. Oh, well, suit yourself," Vance shrugged and withdrew.

The door closed, and Harris returned to his narrative struggles. In less than five minutes the door opened again. The boy tensed.

"I thought you could use a cup of hot chocolate while you wait."

Harris relaxed. "Oh, Jesus, yes! Thanks a lot."

"No trouble." The chocolate was set on the worktable beside Harley's scrawled pages. "The police arrested Sandy Keppler, you know."

"Sandy? But she didn't do it."

"You're sure of that?"

"Positive," said the boy. "There's something I can't quite remember, but I'm sure it's important. Something I heard or saw. I thought if I wrote down every single thing that happened Wednesday morning, maybe it would come back."

"I'm sure it will," said the other. "Perhaps the hot chocolate will help. Better drink it before it gets cold."

"Thanks," said Harley. "You know, you're just about the only person here who's been decent to me. It's really meant a lot."

He removed the lid from the disposable Styrofoam cup, tossed it toward the overflowing wastebasket and lifted the cup to his lips.

"Dammit, Harris!" cried an exasperated Sigrid Harald. She fought her way from behind the batik hanging. "I told you not to drink anything!"

"But it's okay!" he protested, the cup still in midair. "Professor Simpson gave it to me."

Albert Simpson stared at Sigrid in consternation,

then his hand shot out and grasped the cup from Harley's unresisting fingers. Before he could drink, however, the thin young woman wrestled it from his grip. Detective Tildon, who'd been listening at the door ever since Simpson entered the studio, now came up behind the professor and held him immobile as Sigrid carefully retrieved the cup.

It still held a few drops of liquid. More than enough for analysis.

"A trap!" the old man said sadly. "Still, the boy would have told you."

"Told *what?*" wailed Harris. "I didn't see you do anything! I didn't see *anybody* do anything. It was all the lieutenant's idea!"

"I might have known. *Finis coronat opus,*" Simpson said gloomily and declined further speech as Tillie led him away to a waiting squad car.

21

"**B**ut why?" asked Sandy for the third time. Her bright blue eyes still showed traces of crying, but she sat at her own desk once more, and David Wade perched on the edge, holding her hand as if he never meant to let go. They had spent the last half hour in a police car behind the building where they'd waited while the trap was baited and sprung.

"He turned down the chance to be deputy chairman years ago," Sandy said, "and he didn't need the extra salary."

"I don't think money entered into it at all," said Sigrid, leaning against the door frame by the bookcase. One hand held her closed notebook and folder. The other was jammed into the pocket of her unflattering navy-blue slacks.

"No," agreed Nauman from across the wide room. "Not money. His book."

"His *book*?" exclaimed Leyden. "He's been working on that moldy thing for thirty years. What pushed him into action now?"

"The expiration of Wade's contract, probably," said Nauman. "I think he was genuinely fond of you, David."

"He's a great teacher," the young instructor said sadly.

"You're the first in a long time to think so." Nauman's tone was dry. "Most kids today are only interested in the modern. They write their doctorals on obscure German cubists or speculate on missing paintings. But you were fascinated by his Greeks and Romans, *and*," Nauman smiled, "you're almost as bright as Sandy thinks you are. Together you two might well have produced a great book.

"And he had Riley's example. My fault there, I'm afraid, for giving Quinn too much leeway to use Jake as a personal researcher." He glanced at Saxer, who flushed and looked away uncomfortably.

"In any event it made Simpson think he could do the same with you, David, if he were deputy chairman. The way he hated current art trends, he probably felt justified. And maybe he just got fed up with Riley's snide cracks about classical art, and how Bert would never finish his book. Probably all those things combined."

"But did he think I'd stay here with Sandy arrested and everyone thinking she did it for me?" asked David.

"He couldn't have been looking that far ahead when he poisoned Quinn's coffee," said Sigrid. "I think he was truly upset when we arrested Miss Keppler."

"Not half as upset as I was," said David, grinning at Sandy idiotically through his wire-rimmed glasses.

"One little point, though, Miss Keppler," said Tillie curiously. "We could almost have built a real case against you just on that mix-up with Harley Harris's appointment. The dean's secretary—" he consulted his notebook for her name "—Mrs. Meyer, said there was no urgency about the dean's appointment with Professor Nauman that morning, and that she had told you so when she called. It really started to look as if you were trying to crowd this office with people bearing grudges. First Szabo and then Harris. So why didn't you make a later appointment with Mrs. Meyer?"

Sandy's dimples flashed tentatively. "I was afraid of her," she confessed. "I know I shouldn't be, but she and the president's secretary and the dean of administration's secretary eat lunch together every day, and they're very good friends, and—I mean—well, they practically *run* the college."

"The pecking order," said Sigrid, sharing a glance of mutual understanding with Tillie. They both knew how civil service worked, and the girl's reluctance to put off an important dean's secretary was suddenly quite clear.

That part was Greek to Piers Leyden, and he wasn't interested in a translation. "What I *do* want to know is how did Bert do it? Sure, he had plenty of time to doctor Riley's cup while Sandy was in with Vance, but how could he be certain Riley would pick the right one?"

"And what did he think Harley saw?" asked Sandy. "By the time Harley got here, Professor Simpson was back at his desk; and I'm sure he didn't come back in till after Professor Quinn had already taken the cup and gone into his office."

In the last three days Sigrid had listened to many lectures from these professional teachers, and she was not loath to take the lectern herself now.

"It was a matter of good timing and simple sleight of hand," she said. "Remember how Harley Harris sat in this chair right here by the bookcase that held the coffee tray? As someone pointed out, this office is the departmental crossroads, and it's always jammed at the end of the third period. Now Quinn came back from class first, threaded his way through the crowd, picked up a cup and went inside, right?"

Nods and murmurs of assent.

"You were all here," Sigrid said wickedly. "Who was next to take coffee from that tray?"

"Oscar?" someone asked doubtfully.

"Oh!" exclaimed Andrea Ross. Her eyes sparkled with comprehension. "Of course! I even offered to help, but he said he could manage by himself."

"The books!" cried Sandy.

"That's right," said Sigrid. "Immediately after Professor Quinn and just before Professor Nauman, in came Albert Simpson, balancing his still unopened coffee cup on some reference books he was returning to that bookcase. Although he normally seems to have preferred tea, he had ordered coffee with sugar that morning, just like the other two, so there was no difference between his

cup and the others. He set it down on the tray, put the
books on the shelf and then picked up the *other* cup,
which he probably poured down the nearest drain."

"Poison in *both* cups!" said Lemuel Vance. "So it
didn't matter which one Riley picked. I guess old Bert
was smarter than he looked."

"Aren't we all?" said Leyden.

22

Without quite knowing how it happened, Sigrid found herself riding down in the elevator alone with Oscar Nauman. Her awkwardness had returned, and she tried to cover it with a rude remark.

"I hope you have another pipe. That one looks pretty asinine with that wad of adhesive tape."

He ignored it. "I'll pick you up at seven."

"Pick me up for what?"

"Dinner. I've decided we ought to start fresh."

"You've decided—" His gall left her speechless.

"Wear your green suit," he said. "The one with the purple and indigo blouse."

The elevator doors slid open on the ground floor.

"You looked in my closet yesterday? How dare you! That's invasion of privacy!" Indignantly she hurried to catch up with him as he strode down the hall. He held the door for her at the back entrance of Van Hoeen Hall where Detective Tildon waited with the car.

"Seven o'clock," Nauman repeated. "Green suit. And leave your hair loose."

"Be damned if I will!" she said angrily as she slid into the car beside Detective Tildon and banged the door shut.

Tillie looked shocked at her unprecedented display of emotion, but Sigrid ignored his curious face. Never had she met a man so willful, conceited, and infuriating!

Even so, as they drove through the college gates she found herself wondering if she could finish all the reports in time to stop by Anne's apartment and hunt for those jade earrings.

ABOUT THE AUTHOR

Margaret Maron lives with her husband, an artist, on the family farm near Raleigh, North Carolina. ONE COFFEE WITH is the first in her Sigrid Harald series. She is the author of THE RIGHT JACK and BABY DOLL GAMES and is currently working on the sixth Sigrid Harald title, CORPUS CHRISTMAS.

Kinsey Millhone is . . .

"The best new private eye." —The Detroit News

"A tough-cookie with a soft center." —Newsweek

"A stand-out specimen of the new female operatives."
  —Philadelphia Inquirer

Sue Grafton is . . .

The Shamus and Anthony Award-winning creator of Kinsey Millhone and quite simply one of the hottest new mystery writers around.

Bantam is . . .

The proud publisher of Sue Grafton's Kinsey Millhone mysteries:

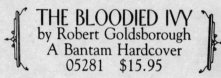

"Ezell Barnes is in the front ranks of the new breed of inner-city Knight Errant."

—Loren D. Estleman
Author of EVERY BRILLIANT EYE

"The inner city is his oyster."

—*New York Magazine*

Easy Does It . . . His Way

Meet Ezell "Easy" Barnes. He's an ex-prizefighter ex-cop p.i. from the gritty streets of Newark, New Jersey. He's tough on crime, wields a wise sense of humor and occasionally thinks with his fists—sometimes that's all there's time for. Not far behind Easy you'll find his best informant—Angel the Sex Change, Newark's diamond in the raunch.

Be sure to read all of the Ezell "Easy" Barnes mysteries by Richard Hillary.